Sealed by a Valentine's Kiss

These untamed docs are almost too hot to handle!

Welcome to Crater Lake, Montana, where doctors Carson and Luke Ralston were born and raised. Big Sky Country gives these gorgeous brothers the space to leave their difficult pasts firmly behind them…
until two new additions to the landscape—feisty surgeon Esme Petersen and east-coast ace Dr Sarah Ledet—upset their careful balance!

Find out what happens in

Carson and Esme's story
His Shock Valentine's Proposal

and

Luke and Sarah's story
Craving Her Ex-Army Doc

Don't miss the *Sealed by a Valentine's Kiss* duet from Mills & Boon Medical Romance author Amy Ruttan

Available from February 2016!

Dear Reader,

Thank you for picking up a copy of *His Shock Valentine's Proposal*.

Montana is a state I never really had on my bucket list. And then one summer, on a drive out to Alberta to visit family, I had the privilege to travel through it. From Broadus to Billings, and up through Great Falls, I fell absolutely head over heels in love. Mountains, sweeping plains and badlands…They say Montana is 'Big Sky Country' and they're right.

After that visit I knew I had to set a story in Montana. Especially in the mountains, nestled against the border of Alberta—a province that was also never on my radar until I had to travel there for my sister-in-law's wedding. I fell in love with Alberta too on that trip.

What struck me about travelling through Montana was its vastness. All that land and barely a person in sight. It's a place to get lost and to find yourself. It's a perfect place for my heroine Esme to hide.

Montana is also a place I wouldn't mind raising my kids. Fresh air, mountains, plains—it's a beautiful land. It's also where my hero grew up. Carson doesn't want to leave Crater Lake, or the family practice he's inherited. And he certainly doesn't want a relationship after his heart is broken. But when he's faced with competition in the form of a new doctor in town maybe love will soften his heart after all?

I love hearing from readers, so please drop by my website, amyruttan.com, or give me a shout on Twitter @ruttanamy.

With warmest wishes,

Amy Ruttan

HIS SHOCK VALENTINE'S PROPOSAL

BY
AMY RUTTAN

First published in Great Britain 2016
By Mills & Boon, an imprint of HarperCollins*Publishers*
1 London Bridge Street, London, SE1 9GF

© 2016 Amy Ruttan

ISBN: 978-0-263-26364-0

Our policy is to use papers that are natural, renewable and recyclable
products and made from wood grown in sustainable forests. The logging
and manufacturing processes conform to the legal environmental
regulations of the country of origin.

Printed and bound in Great Britain
by CPI Antony Rowe, Chippenham, Wiltshire

Born and raised on the outskirts of Toronto, Ontario, **Amy Ruttan** fled the big city to settle down with the country boy of her dreams. Life got in the way, and after the birth of her second child she decided to pursue her dream of becoming a romance author. When she's not furiously typing away at her computer, she's mom to three wonderful children.

Books by Amy Ruttan

Mills & Boon Medical Romance

Safe in His Hands
Melting the Ice Queen's Heart
Pregnant with the Soldier's Son
Dare She Date Again?
It Happened in Vegas
Taming Her Navy Doc
One Night in New York

Visit the Author Profile page at millsandboon.co.uk for more titles.

This book is dedicated to Montana. Your beauty, even four years after I visited you, still haunts me and makes me long to spend endless summers wandering through your mountains, your plains and your badlands.

This book is also for James, who spent his third birthday in Montana on our cross-country trek and loved every second of it. Love you, buddy.

CHAPTER ONE

"WHAT DOES SHE think she's doing?" Carson grumbled to himself.

"Looks like she's planting flowers in a pot," Nurse Adams remarked.

Carson turned and glanced at his father's nurse, who had worked in the practice longer than Carson had. Actually, she was technically his nurse now. He hadn't realized she'd snuck up behind him. Like a ninja.

"I didn't ask for your opinion."

She looked down her nose at him in that way she always did when he was little and causing mischief in his father's office. A look that still sent shivers of dread down his spine and he realized he'd taken it a step too far.

"If you didn't want my opinion, Dr. Ralston, you shouldn't be talking out loud in *my* waiting room."

"Sorry, Louise." He rubbed the back of his neck. "Just hate seeing all these changes going on in Crater Lake."

Her expression softened. "There's a building boom. It was inevitable that another doctor would come into town and set up shop."

Carson frowned and jammed his hands in his trouser pockets as he watched the new, attractive doctor in town planting flowers outside the office across the street. Crater Lake was changing and he wasn't sure he liked it too much.

His father had been the lone physician in Crater Lake for over forty years, long before Carson was born. It was a practice he'd taken over from his grandfather; now Carson had taken over the practice since his parents retired and moved south to warmer climates.

There had always been a Ralston as the town's sole practitioner since Crater Lake was founded in 1908. Something his father liked to remind him of constantly.

The only other time there had been a notion of two town doctors was when Danielle had lived with him for a time after medical school, but that had been different. They were supposed to work together, get married and raise a family. It hadn't lasted. She hadn't liked the slow existence or the winters of living in northwest Montana.

Luke is a doctor.

Carson snorted as he thought of his older brother, who was indeed a licensed practitioner, but Luke didn't like the confines of an office and preferred to be out in the woods tracking bears or whatever he did up on the mountains. Luke didn't have the same passion of upholding the family tradition of having a Ralston as the family practitioner in Crater Lake. That job fell on Carson.

The new doctor in town, Dr. Petersen, stood up, arching her back, stretching. Her blond hair shining in the early summer sunlight. He didn't know much about the newest resident of Crater Lake. Not many people did. She'd moved in and kept to herself. Her practice hadn't even opened yet and though Carson shouldn't care he couldn't help but wonder about her, who she was.

The door jingled and he glanced at the door as his brother came striding in, in his heavy denim and leather, a hank of rope slung around his shoulder.

Louise huffed under her breath as his brother dragged in dirt with his arrival.

"Slow day?" Luke asked as he set the rope down on a chair.

"Yeah. I have the Johnstone twins coming in about an hour for vaccinations."

Luke winced. "I'll be gone before then."

Louise stood up, hands on her ample hips. "Would you pick up that filthy rope? My waiting room was clean until you showed up! Honestly, if your parents were still here…"

Luke chuckled. "You make it sound like they're dead, Louise. They're in Naples, Florida. They live on the edge of a golf course."

Carson chuckled. "Come on, let's retreat to my office. Sorry, Louise."

Carson glanced back one more time, but Dr. Petersen had gone back inside. His brother followed his gaze out the window and then looked at him, confused.

When they were in his office, Luke sat down on one of the chairs. "What was so interesting outside?"

"There's a new doctor in town," Carson said off-handedly.

Luke grinned, leaning back in his chair. "Oh, I see."

"What do you see?"

"I've seen her. I'm not blind."

Carson snorted. "That's not it at all."

Luke cocked an eyebrow. "Then what is it?"

"It's a new doctor in town. It's threatening our family practice."

Luke shrugged. "It's your practice, not mine."

So like his brother. Not caring much about the family practice. Not caring about generations of Ralstons who'd sweated to build this practice and this town up. Well, at least he cared.

Do you?

Carson pinched the bridge of his nose. "I thought you were against the town expansion and the building of that ski-resort community."

"I am. Well...I was, but really there was no stopping it."

"You could've attended a few town meetings," Carson said.

When had Luke stopped caring so much?

It wasn't his concern and by the way Luke was glaring at him Carson was crossing a line. His brother quickly changed the subject. "I guess my point was that it didn't look like you were checking out the competition the way you want me to think you were."

"I'll work that out later." Carson moved around and sat down on the other side of his desk. "What brings you down off the mountain and what in heaven's name are you going to tie up with that rope?"

Luke grinned in the devilish way that used to cause their mother to worry. It usually meant that Luke was about to get into some serious trouble.

"Nothing much. I actually just came for some medical supplies. I'm taking some surveyors deep into the woods."

"And the rope is to tie them to the nearest tree and use them as bear bait?"

"The thought had crossed my mind, but like you,

little brother, I took the Hippocratic Oath. I swore to do no harm."

"Hmm."

"You need to liven up a bit, little brother. You're too tense."

Carson snorted. "Look who's talking. You know the local kids refer to you as the Grinch in the winter. One of the Johnstone twins thought you were going to come down and steal Christmas last year."

"Because I told her that. She spooked my horse."

"You're terrible with kids and have a horrible bed-side manner," Carson said.

"I'm great with kids. Dad just knew you were more of the office type of person and I like to run wild."

Must be nice.

The thought surprised him, because he should be used to Luke's lifestyle after all this time. Luke always got to run free, do what he wanted. Carson was the re-liable one.

Dependable.

Never took risks.

Carson shook his head. "As long as you're not naked while running wild then I don't care."

Luke grinned. "I didn't know how much you cared."

Carson couldn't help but chuckle. "You need to get your butt out of my clean office before you give Louise a heart attack and get yourself back up that mountain. I have patients coming in soon. Patients who think you're going to steal their Christmas."

"Right. So, do I get the medical supplies? I may not have regular office time but I technically have part ownership."

"You know where they are. I don't have to tell you."

"Thanks." Luke got up.

"Take your rope, too."

Luke winked and disappeared into the stockroom while Carson leaned back in his father's chair and scrubbed a hand over his face.

Luke had one thing right. He was tense. He worked too much.

You're wasting your surgical talent here. Why didn't you take that internship at Mayo? Why are you giving up a prestigious surgical residency to become a general practitioner?

Danielle's words haunted him.

Lately, they had been bothering him more. Ever since the old office building across the road had been bought and he'd got wind that a new doctor from Los Angeles was moving into town. There weren't many full-timers in Crater Lake. The ageing population was a threat to the small town and now with this resort community going in, it would bring more people, but not people who would be here all the time and Carson couldn't help but wonder if the time of the small-town doctor was gone.

Perhaps he had wasted his life? Maybe he should've cared less about the practice like Luke. Maybe he would've become a great surgeon.

More and more lately it seemed he was thinking these thoughts. He didn't take risks, but he was happy with the choices he made.

This was the path he chose and he was happy.

He was happy.

Who are you trying to convince?

He groaned inwardly. He didn't have to let the ghosts of his past haunt him.

Get a grip on yourself.

Carson shook those thoughts away.

No, he was doing what he'd always wanted to do. Sure, he'd been offered several amazing residencies, but surgery was not what he wanted to do.

He liked the small-town life; he liked the connection he had with the people in Crater Lake. He would be stifled in a big city; he'd be trapped in a busy hospital in the OR for countless hours. This he preferred.

Still...

It irked him that another doctor had moved into town, but he couldn't stop it and frankly he hoped she was up to the challenge. She was from California. He doubted it very much that she would be able to survive her first winter here and that thought secretly pleased him.

Louise knocked and then opened his door. She looked worried. "Dr. Ralston, Mrs. Johnstone is in the waiting room. She needs to speak with you."

"Is everything okay? I thought the twins' appointment was later?"

Louise's lips pursed together. "She's here to cancel her appointment and take their chart."

"Hold on!" Esme called out. She had no idea who was banging on the front door of her office. She wasn't open yet. The big day was at the end of the week. If it was a delivery they could've read the sign and come along to the back alleyway.

Only the banging was insistent. It sounded almost angry, which made her pause. Perhaps she should take a peek out the window. The last thing she wanted was it to be the tabloids outside pounding on her door. Not that they'd bothered with her for the past three months.

She'd dealt with enough press in LA before she'd

hightailed it to the solitude of the mountains. Of course, when she'd chosen Crater Lake as her new home, she'd known that there was going to be a resort community, but she hadn't realized another high-end spa and hotel was going up.

Esme could handle a small ski-resort community, but a huge high-end spa and hotel? That was not what she wanted. Small. Sleepy and in need of a friendly and eager town physician. Of course, once she'd spent all her money on buying her practice she really hadn't been able to change her mind. The building she had bought had been on the market for five years.

She knew there was an *old* family practice in town. Dr. Ralston had been practicing medicine in Crater Lake his whole career and his father before that and his father before that. It was time to breathe some new life into Crater Lake.

The pounding reminded her why her inventory of medical supplies was being interrupted and she glanced out of the window of her primary exam room.

"Whoa."

The handsome man standing in front of her office was definitely not paparazzi or press. He didn't have a camera or a recorder, or even a smartphone on him. He was well dressed in casual business attire. His brown hair combed neatly, clean shaven, but definitely an outdoorsy type of guy, because she could see his forearms where he'd rolled up the sleeves of his crisp white shirt were tanned and muscular.

He was a well-dressed country boy and Esme had a thing for country boys. Always had, but that was a hard thing to find in Los Angeles.

Unless you counted the country singers she'd treated,

and she didn't. Of course, when she'd thought she'd found the perfect guy it had turned out she hadn't and she was terrified by who she'd become and about what he wanted from her.

Don't think about Shane.

Well, whoever this guy was, he was off-limits. She wasn't here to get involved with anyone. Besides, he was probably married or taken. One thing Esme had discovered about her new place of residence was that Crater Lake was mostly filled with older people and young families. It wasn't a happening place for singles and that was fine by her.

She was here to hide, not find happiness. She didn't deserve that. Not after what she'd done to Shane.

Not after what happened in the OR with her last surgery. It was too painful. Love and friendship, they were not what she was here for. She was here to be a doctor. She was here to blend in, to hide so no one could find her.

He banged on the door again.

She ran her hand through her hair, hoping she didn't smell of sweat too much. Even though she had no interest in impressing him, she didn't want to scare off any potential patients because she gave off the impression of being smelly.

"Just a minute!" Esme called out as she undid the chain and bolt on her office door. She opened it. "Hey, look, I'm not open today."

"I'm aware," he said tersely. "Can I come in?"

"I don't even know you."

"Is that how you plan to treat residents of Crater Lake?" he asked.

What's this guy's deal?

"Okay, how about we start with introductions? I'm Dr. Petersen." She held out her hand, but he just glanced at it, ignoring her proffering.

"I know who you are, Dr. Petersen." His blue eyes were dark, his brow furrowed.

Oh, crap.

"You do? You know who I am? I'm sorry I can't say the same."

He was clearly annoyed and she didn't have time for this. "Look, I'm kind of busy today. Why don't you call my office and my nurse will call you about an appointment time? I'm pretty open for appointments as I'm not open for business just yet."

"You have a nurse?" he asked.

"Well, not yet, but I've interviewed some interesting candidates."

"I bet."

Esme frowned. "Have I offended you some way? If I have, I'm really sorry, but again I haven't opened yet."

"I'm aware you're not open yet. Of course, that really doesn't stop you from poaching patients."

Esme was stunned. "Who are you?"

"I'm Dr. Ralston. I was the Johnstone family's practitioner up until about two hours ago."

Okay, now she was really surprised. "You're Dr. Ralston?"

"Yes."

"Dr. C. Ralston?"

"Yes."

"I don't get it." Esme stepped aside to invite him in, but didn't even get the words out as he wandered inside and then sat on the edge of the waiting-room desk, his arms crossed.

"What don't you get? I can show you my ID."

"Dr. Charles Ralston has been practicing medicine in Crater Lake for forty years." She shut the door, but didn't lock it just in case this guy was crazy or something. "You guys either have the fountain of youth up here in Crater Lake or someone's records are incorrect."

A small smile played on his face, some of that fury fading. "Dr. Charles Ralston is my father. I'm Dr. Carson Ralston. I took over my father's practice when he retired five years ago."

"Oh, and I'm the fool who just poached some of your patients. Gotcha."

"Essentially."

Esme crossed her arms, too. "So how can I help you?"

"Stop poaching my patients." There was now a slight twinkle in his blue, blue eyes and he didn't seem as angry anymore.

"I'm really sorry, but your patient wanted to change. I couldn't turn them away," she stated.

"Look, you have to know when you come to a small town you don't go around stealing the patients of a practitioner who has been here for quite some time."

Esme raised an eyebrow. "Is that some kind of doctor rule? If so, I'm not aware of it."

"It's common courtesy." He didn't seem as though he was going to budge until she handed over the files to him. Although, she hadn't been given the files yet.

"I'm sorry to disappoint you, Dr. Ralston, but when I bumped into Mrs. Johnstone at the general store her twins took a shine to me and she wanted me to be her physician."

"What do you mean the twins took a shine to you?"

She grinned. "I mean I didn't scare them like the old, grumpy Dr. Ralston."

His mouth fell open in surprise for a moment and then he snapped it shut. "Okay, then. I won't bother you about it anymore."

"That's quite the defeatist attitude."

He shrugged and headed to the door. "If I'm old and grumpy then there is nothing more I can do."

A sense of dread niggled at her. "What do you know about them you're not sharing?"

Now it was his turn to grin with pleasure. "Nothing. Just good luck with the twins, but I will tell you that if you take any more of my patients it'll be war."

Esme couldn't help but laugh. "Are you declaring war on me, Dr. Ralston?"

"I believe I am, Dr. Petersen." He winked, chuckling to himself as he shut the door behind him and Esme couldn't help but wonder what she'd gotten herself into. She would have to keep her distance from Carson, though in a small town that was going to be hard to do, but she was going to try.

CHAPTER TWO

CARSON WAS GLAD that summer was coming, the days were longer, but then he really couldn't enjoy the extra daylight when he stayed late and he usually stayed late because he didn't have anything to go home to.

He had a big empty house that he used for sleeping. That was it. He'd built it for Danielle and him. Of course Danielle hadn't stayed long enough to live in it.

The sun was just beginning to set behind the mountains, giving a pink tinge to the glacier on Mount Jackson. He never got tired of it. He loved Montana and if he did have regrets about his past, staying in Montana wasn't one of them.

Still, the mountains, the scenery weren't any kind of companion, but at least the mountains would never betray him and wouldn't break his heart the way Danielle had done.

As he locked up the clinic he couldn't help but glance across the street at Dr. Petersen's clinic. The lights were still blazing. She'd opened at the end of last week, but Carson hadn't lost any more patients. Most of her patients seemed to be coming down from the resort community and with that new high-end hotel and spa going in there would be even more people coming.

There were a few timeshares that were in operation, but he knew the main lodge was still under construction, as his brother was still taking surveyors and construction workers out on the trails.

Once the main spa hotel lodge opened and the community got its own full-time doctor, a job he'd turned down, then Dr. Petersen might feel a bit of pain financially.

A twinge of guilt ate at him and he felt bad for declaring war on her.

"You declared war on her? How does that even happen?" Luke had had a good laugh over that.

Of course, the last time Carson had declared war on someone was when Luke and he had been kids. Carson had declared war on Luke when he was ten and Luke had been fifteen. Carson had gone about booby-trapping parts of the house. The ceasefire had come when Luke had set a snare and Carson had ended up dangling upside down in a tree with a sign that said bear food.

Their father had put a stop to all present and future wars.

Carson sighed. He hadn't been thinking that day in her surgery. She got on his nerves a bit and he had been put out that the Johnstone twins had thought he was grumpy and old. He honestly was glad to be rid of the little hellions.

It was the principle of the matter.

In all the years his father had practiced he'd never been called grumpy or old. He'd never lost a patient to another doctor.

There never was another doctor in Crater Lake.

A lot of new families had come into town over the past couple of years. Dr. Petersen was advertising. He'd heard her ad on the local radio station. Perhaps he needed to advertise. Maybe he was a bit too comfortable in his position and he was in a rut.

Carson rubbed the back of his neck.

He should go make amends with her.

He crossed the street and peered inside the clinic window to see if he could catch sight of her, get her attention, then maybe he could talk to her.

Before he knew what was happening there was a shout, his wrist was grabbed and he was on the ground staring at the pavement.

"What in the heck?" Carson shouted as a pain shot up his arm. He craned his neck to see Esme Petersen, sitting on his back, holding his left wrist, which was wrenched in an awkward position behind him. "Um, you can let go of me. I kind of need my arm."

"Oh, my gosh. Dr. Ralston, I'm so sorry." She let go of his wrist and got off his back. "I thought you were a burglar."

Carson groaned and heaved himself up off the pavement. "There aren't many burglars around Crater Lake. It's a pretty safe town."

"I'm really sorry for attacking you like that, but you scared me. Why the heck were you skulking around the outside of my office?"

"How the heck did you do that?" Carson asked, smoothing out his shirt.

"Do what?" Esme asked.

"Take me down?"

Esme grinned. "Krav Maga."

Carson frowned. "Never heard of it. What is it?"

Esme shook her head. "You still haven't answered my question. Why were you peering through the windows and generally acting suspicious? This doesn't have to do with the *war*, does it?"

"Kind of." Carson touched his forehead and winced. "I think I'm bleeding."

"Oh, my God. You are." Esme took his hand and led him to the open door. "Come inside and I'll clean that up. It's the least I can do."

"No, thank you," Carson murmured, trying to take his hand back. "I think you've done enough damage."

"No way. You owe me this." She dragged him into her very bright and yellow clinic waiting room. It was cheery and it made him wince. "You can head into the exam room and I'll take a look at the damage."

Carson snorted. "Are you going to charge me a fee?"

Esme rolled her eyes. "So petulant. I just may, since you were creeping around in the shadows trying to scare me."

Carson sat on the exam table as she came bustling into the room and then washed her hands in the sink, her small delicate hands. They looked soft, warm, and he wondered how they would feel in his. He couldn't think that way.

"I wasn't trying to scare you," he said.

"You said it was about the war you declared on me. Doesn't that usually involve trickery and scaring tactics?" Esme stood on her tiptoes and tried to get a box from a high shelf. She started cursing and mumbling under her breath as she couldn't quite reach it.

Carson stood and reached up, getting the box of gauze for her, his fingers brushing hers as she still tried to reach for it.

So soft.

His heart raced, he was standing so close to her,

and he looked down at her and she stared up at him in shock that he'd done that for her. He hadn't realized how blue her eyes were or how red her lips were and the color was accentuated by the white-blond of her hair. She kind of reminded him of a short, feisty Marilyn Monroe.

Focus.

Carson moved his hand away and tossed her the box of gauze. "If you can't reach it, you shouldn't put it up so high."

"I didn't. My nurse did. He is a bit taller than me."

"He?" Carson asked, teasing her.

"Sexist, too, are we?"

"Please."

"Sit down. You're such a whiner, Dr. Ralston."

Carson sat back on the table; his head was throbbing now. "Dang, you did a number on me. What did you call that again?"

"Krav Maga." Esme pulled on gloves. "Sorry."

"No, it's fine. You're right. I shouldn't have been... what did you call it?"

"Skulking." She smiled, her eyes twinkling as she parted his hair to look at his injury.

Carson winced again, ignoring the sting. It wasn't the sting that bothered him, it was her touch. Just the sudden contact sent a zing through him. It surprised him. It was unwelcome. He wanted to move away from her, so he wasn't so close, but that was hard to do when she was cleaning up his wound. "Right. Skulking. I shouldn't have been doing that outside your office."

She nodded and began to clean the wound. "So why were you?"

"I came to apologize."

Her eyes widened. "Oh, really?"

"Yeah. I shouldn't have come barging over here and accusing you of stealing my patients."

"So are you calling a truce?"

"I am. Ow."

Esme *tsked* under her breath. "It's just a scrape. Don't be such a baby."

"Do you talk to all your patients this way?"

"Only ones who whine so much." She smiled and continued to dab at his scrape. "There. I'll just put some ointment on it. Do you want a bandage?"

"No, thanks."

Esme shrugged and then rubbed some antiseptic ointment on the scrape.

"Ow."

"Doctors are the worst patients," she muttered.

"For a reason." Carson chuckled.

"I've never really understood that reason." She pulled off her gloves and tossed them in the medical-waste receptacle. "There. All done."

"Thanks."

"Are you sure you don't want a bandage? Maybe a pressure dressing." She was chuckling to herself and he rolled his eyes.

"Pretty sure." Carson sighed. He had to get out of the clinic before something else happened. Such as him doing something irrational. Only he couldn't move. "I better be going. Again, I'm really sorry for being such an idiot before."

She grinned. "Apology accepted."

Esme didn't really know what else to say. She felt very uncomfortable around Carson, but not in a bad way. In a very good way and that was dangerous. When their hands had barely touched a few moments ago, it had sent a zing through her. One that wasn't all that unpleasant. Actually, it had been some time since she'd felt that spark with someone. Of course, relationships never worked out for her. Men couldn't handle her drive and focus to commit to surgery and she had liked her independence and career too much. No one messed with her career.

Well, not anymore. She couldn't forget why she was a surgeon.

Hold on, Avery. Please.

Let me go, little sister. It hurts so much...let me go.

She'd dedicated her life to surgery. To save lives.

And until Shane, surgery had been her life. Her father had been so proud and she'd been training under Dr. Eli Draven, the best cardio-thoracic surgeon on the West Coast.

She'd thrown herself into her work. So much so, that she hadn't had time to date, until Eli had introduced her to his son.

She'd met Shane and surgery had become second, because he had always been taking her somewhere. Esme had been swept off her feet and, being the protégée of Dr. Eli Draven, she'd become too cocky. Too sure of herself. She'd thought she'd had it all.

Then in a routine procedure, she'd frozen. A resident had jumped in, knocking sense back into her and they'd worked hard to save the patient's life. But in the end they'd lost the fight.

Esme hadn't been able to go on, because in that moment—in that failure—she'd realized that she didn't know who she was anymore. She didn't know who she'd become, but it wasn't her.

Pulled back from her memories, Esme stared down at her hands, watching how they shook.

You're not a surgeon anymore, she reminded herself.

She'd come here to rebuild her life and right now she should be focusing on building her practice up, because every last dime of her savings had been sunk into this building. She'd bought the clinic, the license and the apartment upstairs.

This was her life now. She didn't have a retired parent to hand off a practice to her. Her stepmother had been a teacher and her father a cop.

They'd scrimped and saved to send her to the best medical school. Scholarships only went so far and she owed it to them to pay them back, since she could no longer be the surgeon they expected her to be.

She'd lost herself.

And she'd lost Shane. If only she'd come to the realization that he wasn't the man for her *before* she was in her wedding dress and halfway down the aisle on Valentine's Day. It was something she had to live with for the rest of her life.

Her father had made that clear to her. He'd been so disappointed. She'd let him down.

I don't know who you are anymore, Esme.

She didn't deserve any kind of happiness, or friendship. All she deserved was living with herself. Living with the stranger she'd become.

"Well, I have a bit of work to do tomorrow. I better

hit the hay," she said awkwardly, rubbing the back of her neck and trying not to look at him.

"Yeah, of course. I…" Carson said, trying to excuse himself when there was banging on her front door. Incessant and urgent.

"Who in the world?"

"Just stay here." Carson pushed her down into her chair, letting her know that he wanted her to stay put, before he headed out to the front door.

"As if," she mumbled, following him.

"I told you to stay in the exam room," he whispered as he stood in front of the door.

She crossed her arms. "You don't know Krav Maga. I do."

He rolled his eyes. "Fine."

Esme stood on her tiptoes and peered around him. When he opened the door a man let out a sigh of relief.

"Thank God I found you, Doc Ralston."

"Harry, what's wrong?" Carson asked, stepping aside to let the man in.

The man, Harry, was sweating and dirty, dressed in heavy denim, with thick work boots and leaving a trail of wood chips on her floor. He nodded to her. "Dr. Petersen."

"How can we help you…Harry, is it?"

"Yes, ma'am." He was twisting a ball cap in his hands and it looked as if he was in shock. "There's been an accident at Bartholomew's Mill."

"An accident?" Carson asked. "What kind?"

"Jenkins had a nasty incident with a saw, but there's bad smoke from a remote forest fire and we can't get a chopper in to airlift him to a hospital and paramedics are still two hours away."

Esme reeled at that information. She knew they were far off the beaten path, but medical help was two hours away? Why wasn't there a hospital closer?

"Let's go. I'll go grab my emergency medical kit." Carson slapped Harry on the shoulder. "I hope you don't mind driving, Harry. You know those logging roads better than me in the dark."

"No problem, Dr. Ralston."

"Can I help?" Esme asked.

Carson nodded. "Grab as many suture kits as you can."

Esme panicked. "Hospitals take care of suturing. We're not surgeons."

Carson shook his head. "Not around here. I hope you have some surgical skills. We're going to need them."

Harry and Carson disappeared into the night. Esme's stomach twisted in a knot. Suturing? Surgery? This wasn't what she'd signed up for.

When she'd moved here she'd put that all behind her. She wasn't a surgeon.

No.

Then she thought of Avery. Her brother bleeding out under her hands. She was being foolish. They needed her help. Someone was in pain. This wasn't an OR. She would make sure she wouldn't freeze up. She wouldn't. She couldn't. This was about sustaining a man's life until paramedics arrived. Esme rushed into her supply room, grabbed a rucksack and began to pack it full of equipment. Her hands shaking as she grabbed the suture kit.

I can do this.

Besides, she might not even have to stitch him.

Carson could handle it and nothing was going to happen.

This man wouldn't die.

This wasn't a surgery case. At least she hoped it wasn't.

CHAPTER THREE

ESME BIT HER lip in worry as they slowly traversed some windy hills up into the mountains. At least that was what she assumed by the bumps and the climbs that tried the engine of Harry's truck. She couldn't see anything.

She'd thought she knew what pitch-black was.

The sky was full of clouds and smoke from a forest fire, which Carson had assured her wasn't any threat to them. California had wild fires, but not really in Los Angeles, at least not when she was there. Then again, she wasn't a native Californian.

Fire, wilderness, bears, this existence was all new to her, but then this was what she wanted after all. This was a big wide place she could easily blend in. She was small here. A place she could hide, because who in their right mind would come looking for her here?

A large bump made her grip the dashboard tighter. She was wedged between Harry and Carson as they took the logging road deep into the camp.

Another bump made her hiss and curse under her breath.

Carson glanced at her. "You're mighty tense."

"Just hoping we don't die."

Harry chuckled. "We're not on the edge of a cliff. Our only threat is maybe a rock slide or a logging truck careening down the road, but since there are no trucks running we're pretty safe."

"I'll keep telling myself that we're safe, Harry."

He shook his head, probably at the folly of a city girl. Only it was a dark night like this when Avery had died. She'd only been ten years old, but the memory of her brother's gaping chest wound was still fresh. The feel of his exposed heart under her small hands, the warmth of his blood felt fresh. It was why she'd wanted to be a cardio-thoracic surgeon.

Why she'd worked so hard to be the best, because Avery had been a constant in her parents' strained marriage. Even though he'd been twelve years older than her.

He'd been her best friend and when he'd died, her world had been shattered. So she'd dedicated her life to surgery.

The nightmares of his death faded away but nights like this made it all rush back.

Carson slipped an arm around her shoulders and then leaned over. "Relax. You're okay."

She glanced at his arm around hers and she wanted to shrug it off, but it felt good there. Reassuring. It made her feel safe and she wished she could snuggle in. Esme let out the breath she hadn't realized she'd been holding in trepidation and leaned back against the seat, shrugging off Carson's arm. She could handle this. Alone.

"So what happened again, Harry?" Carson asked.

"Jenkins was overtired and nervous. Our new client, Mr. Draven, was headed out our way tomorrow. One wrong move and..." Harry trailed off.

Esme froze at the mention of the name Draven.
Dammit.

Though it couldn't be Dr. Draven, her former mentor. Eli was a cardio-thoracic surgeon. Still the name sent dread down her spine.

Draven was a common name. So there was no way it would be Eli or Shane. Dr. Draven had money, but he invested it in medicine and science. All of Shane's money was tied up in his company. She doubted he would invest in lumber or a hotel in Montana.

Harry slowed the truck down and she could see light through the trees as the forest thinned out. There were floodlights everywhere and people milling around one of the buildings, which looked like an administrative building. Harry pulled up right in front of it.

Carson opened the door and jumped out, reaching into the back to grab their supplies. Esme followed suit, trying to ignore all the eyes on them as they made their way into the building. The moment the door opened they could hear a man screaming in pain.

Esme forgot all the trepidation about anyone recognizing her. That all melted away. Adrenaline fueled her now as she headed toward the man in pain. There was blood, but it wasn't the damage done by the saw that caught her attention. It was his neck, and as she bent over the man she could see the patient's neck veins were bulging as he struggled, or rather as his heart struggled to beat. Only it was drowning.

She'd seen it countless times when she was a resident surgeon, before she'd chosen her specialty. Before she'd become a surgeon to the stars. First she had to confirm the rest of Beck's Triad, before she even thought about trying to right it.

She didn't want to freeze up. Not here. Not in her new start.

"Dave, you're going to be fine," Carson said, trying to soothe the patient. Only Dave Jenkins couldn't hear him. "It doesn't look like he's lost a lot of blood."

"He's lost blood," she said, trying not to let her voice shake.

Just not externally.

Carson took off his jacket, rolling up his sleeves to inspect the gash on Dave's right arm. "It's deep, but hasn't severed any arteries."

The wound had been put in a tourniquet, standard first aid from those trained at the mill. It wasn't bleeding profusely. It would need cleaning and a few stitches to set it right.

"That's not the problem." Esme pulled out her stethoscope.

Carson cocked an eyebrow. "Really?"

"Really." She peered down at Dave. His faceplate, his eyes rolling back into his head. He was in obstructive shock. "Who saw what happened? There's more than a gash to the arm going on here."

"A piece of timber snapped back and hit Dave here." Esme glanced up as the man pointed to his sternum.

"The gash came after?" she asked.

"No, before, but Dave didn't get out of the way and he didn't shut off the machine after the first malfunction. He was overtired—"

"Got it." Esme cut him off. She bent over and listened. The muffled heart sounds were evident. A wall of blood drowning out the rhythmic diastole and systole of the heart. Drowning it. Cursing under her breath, she quickly took his blood pressure, but she knew when the man pointed to his sternum what was wrong.

Cardiac tamponade.

Dave wouldn't survive the helicopter coming. He probably wouldn't have survived the trip to the hospital.

"What's his blood pressure?" Carson asked.

"Ninety over seventy. He's showing signs of Beck's Triad."

"Cardiac tamponade?"

Esme nodded and rifled through her rucksack, finding the syringe she needed and alcohol to sterilize. "I have to aspirate the fluid from around his heart."

"Without an ultrasound?" Carson asked. "How can...? Only trained trauma surgeons can do that."

Esme didn't say anything. She wasn't a trauma surgeon, though she worked in an ER during her residency. She'd done this procedure countless times. She was, after all, the cardio God. She knew the heart. It was her passion, her reason for living. She loved everything about the heart. She loved its complexities, its mysteries.

She knew the heart. She loved the heart.

Or at least she had.

"It's okay. I've done this before. Once."

She was lying. She'd done this countless times. She'd learned the procedure from Dr. Draven. It was a signature move of his that he taught only a select few, but they didn't need to know that. How many general practitioners performed this procedure multiple times? Not many.

"Once?"

"I really don't have time to explain. It's preferable to have an ultrasound, but we don't have one. I need to do this or he'll die. Open his shirt."

Carson cut the shirt open, exposing Dave's chest where a bruise was forming on the sternum.

You can do this.

"I need two men to hold him in case he jerks, and he can't. Not when I'm guiding a needle into the sac around his heart."

There were a couple of gasps, but men stepped forward, holding the unconscious Dave down.

Esme took a deep breath, swabbed the skin and then guided the needle into his chest. She visualized the pericardial sac in her head, remembering from the countless times she'd done this every nuance of the heart and knowing when to stop so she didn't penetrate the heart muscle. She pulled back on the syringe and it filled with blood, the blood that was crushing the man's heart. The blood that the heart should've been pumping through with ease, but instead was working against him, to kill him.

Carson watched Esme in amazement. He'd never encountered Beck's Triad before. Well, not since his fleeting days as an intern. It was just something he didn't look for as a family practitioner. Cardiac tamponade was usually something a trauma surgeon saw because a cardiac tamponade was usually caused by an injury to the heart, by blunt force, gunshot or stab wound.

Those critical cases in Crater Lake, not that there were many, were flown out to the hospital. How did Esme know how to do that? It became clear to Carson that she hadn't been a family practitioner for very long. She was a surgeon before, but why was she hiding it?

Why would she hide such a talent?

It baffled him.

Because as he watched her work, that was what he saw. Utter talent as she drained the pericardial sac with ease. She then smiled as she listened with her stethoscope.

"Well?" Carson asked, feeling absolutely useless.

"He'll make it to the hospital, but he'll need a CT and possibly surgery depending on the extent of his injuries."

There was a whir of helicopter blades outside and Harry came running in. "The medics are here to fly him to the hospital."

Esme nodded. "I'll go talk to them. Pack the wound on his arm."

Carson just nodded and watched her as she disappeared outside with Harry. She was so confident and sure of herself. She had been when he'd first met her, but this was something different. It reminded him of Danielle. Whenever she was on the surgical floor Danielle was a totally different person.

Actually, Carson found most surgeons to be arrogant and so sure of everything they did, but then they'd have to be. Lives were in their hands. Not that lives weren't in his hands, but it was a different scale.

Carson rarely dealt with the traumatic.

He turned to Dave's wound and cleansed it, packing it with gauze to protect it on his journey to the nearest hospital.

Esme rounded the corner and behind her were two paramedics. He could still hear the chopper blades rotating; they were going to pack him and get out fast, before smoke from the forest fires blew back in this direction and inhibited their takeoff.

Esme was still firing off instructions as they carefully loaded Dave onto their stretcher and began to hook up an IV and monitors to him. Carson helped slip on the oxygen mask. They moved quick, and he followed them outside as they ran with the gurney to the waiting chopper.

Esme stood back beside him, her arm protecting her face from the dust kicking up. There was no room on the chopper for them and they weren't needed anymore. The paramedics could handle Dave and he'd soon be in the capable hands of the surgeons at the hospital.

As the door to the chopper slammed it began to lift above the mill, above the thinned forest and south toward the city. Once the helicopter was out of sight, Esme sighed.

"Well, that was more excitement than I was preparing for tonight."

"You were amazing in there," Carson stated. "Was your previous general practice in a large city? I rarely see cardiac tamponades in my clinic. Or did you work at a hospital under a cardio-thoracic surgeon? The way you handled that I'm surprised you didn't become a cardio-thoracic surgeon. You had the steady hand of an experienced surgeon."

Esme's eyes widened and she bit her lip, before shrugging. "Sure, yeah, a cardio-thoracic surgeon mentor. So where's Harry gone? I really want to get back home. It's getting late. I better get my things."

She turned and headed back into the building, her arms wrapped tight around her lithe body.

Carson sighed and followed her and helped her clean up. She didn't engage him in any further discussion about the matter. They just disposed of soiled material and bagged up the rest of their stuff.

"Docs, I have the truck ready. I can take you back to town now," Harry said as he wandered into the room.

"Thanks, Harry." Carson glanced at Esme, who seemed to have relaxed and returned to herself. "You ready to go, Dr. Petersen?"

"Yes. I'm exhausted!" She smiled. "Thanks for taking us back to town, Harry."

Harry shrugged. "It's no problem. I don't stay up here at the camp. I'm local."

"Oh, you're local, all right, Harry," Carson teased as he picked up his bag. Harry just chuckled and they followed him out of the admin building to his pickup truck.

Now that the excitement had died down, workers were headed back to their bunks or back to the mill to work. He could hear the saws starting up again.

Esme climbed into the middle and Carson slid in beside her.

Harry turned the ignition and then rolled down his window, to lean his elbow out the side. "Yeah, the guys are a bit stressed around here. Mr. Draven is coming here tomorrow morning to inspect the mill. It's got the boss Bartholomew on edge. With the Draven contract for his resort that will mean a lot of work. A lot of money."

"What's Mr. Draven's first name?" There was an edge to Esme's voice.

"Silas. He's a big hotel mogul from out east," Harry said.

"East?" There was a bit of relief in her voice.

"Do you know Mr. Draven?" Carson asked.

"N-no. Just heard of him. The name sounded familiar, but I don't know Silas Draven."

Somehow Carson knew that was a lie, just by the nervous tone to Esme's voice and the way she'd sounded so relieved.

"He's never come to the mill before," Harry remarked. "I mean, he's a big rich investor. Doesn't know much about lumber mills other than what his advisors tell him, but I suspect it has something to do with competing. There's untapped tourist resources."

"Another hotel?" Carson asked.

Great.

It was supposed to be a simple resort community. Small and unique. Every time he heard something new about it, it was spiraling out of control. Perhaps it was the competitors that Luke had been taking up into the mountains to do surveying. More change.

Change can be good.

Only he didn't believe that. Change only brought heartache, disaster.

Temptation.

And he glanced over at Esme, sitting beside him in the dark. She was definitely a temptation.

"You okay?" she asked.

"Fine."

"You're scowling."

"I'm not. Besides, how can you tell? It's pitch-black out there."

"There's a moon and the dashboard light."

Indeed, in the flicker of light he could see her smiling at him, her eyes twinkling in the dark, and he couldn't help but smile, even though he didn't feel like it at the moment. Even though he knew nothing about her, being around her tonight had been a bit magical. It had been exciting and he couldn't remember the last time he'd felt such a rush.

Don't think about her like that.

"Do you think Dave will make it?" Harry asked, breaking through his thoughts.

"He should. Once he's in the hands of a capable cardio-thoracic surgeon." Esme leaned against the seat. "Which I'm not."

"You said that with such force," Carson said. "You really want to be clear that you're not a cardio-thoracic surgeon."

Her smile disappeared. "Because I'm not. I'm just lucky enough to have had the chance to perform that a couple of times."

"I thought it was only once?"

Esme stiffened. "Once was an understatement."

"Clearly, because the way you executed that procedure was superb. In fact, it looked like you'd been doing that for quite some time. Especially since you executed it without the use of an ultrasound."

Esme snorted. "I'm just a general practitioner and I did what I had to do to save a man's life. Can we drop the interrogation?"

"I'm not interrogating you."

She shrugged. "I've told you I've done it a couple of times. I guess I was lucky—really there was no other choice. Dave would've died had I not performed it then and there."

"You're right. Let's drop it."

"Good."

Carson turned and looked out the window, not that there was anything to see in the dark, on a logging road, in the middle of the forest, but he didn't feel like engaging in small talk with Esme. She was maddening.

It was clear to Carson by the way she wasn't looking at him and the way her body became tense that she wasn't too keen on discussing the matter further. What was she hiding?

Why do you care?

Perhaps because he'd been duped by a female before.

Working at your dad's practice sounds great! I would love to.

Then of course Danielle's tune had changed.

This is never what I wanted. You didn't give me much of a choice.

Not that he should care if Esme was lying to him. Let her have her secrets. It didn't matter. They weren't involved, they weren't colleagues and they certainly weren't friends. They were just two doctors in the same, sleepy small town.

That was it.

CHAPTER FOUR

ESME MANAGED TO avoid Carson for two weeks after working up on the mountain. She just decided it was in everyone's best interest if she laid low. Less questions to be asked that way. She knew Carson didn't believe her lies.

Great.

Why did that accident have to happen in front of Carson? She was here to be a simple physician. Not a surgeon, but then if she hadn't been there, Dave would've died. He wouldn't have made it to the hospital.

So she'd done the right thing, even if it had meant she'd had to perform a surgical procedure in front of Carson. Something she'd sworn she wasn't going to do when she got to Crater Lake.

The best solution was to avoid Carson for a while.

Which was why Esme was standing in the produce section of a big chain grocery store two towns away, staring at a pile of cantaloupes.

Run.

That was what she was telling herself, or at least the cowardly voice in her head was telling her.

Where?

That she didn't know. She couldn't go home to her

father. He'd made it clear that her running away was not the answer. That was what her mother had done. After Avery's death, she'd packed up and run away.

I've been a wife and mother. It's time for me. I gave up my life for you.

It had broken her father's heart. He'd lost a son and wife in the same year.

Now a daughter.

Ever since she'd left Los Angeles her father had made it clear how disappointed he was in her, so she was the last person her father wanted to see. She was just a big failure.

"Nice melons."

Esme shook her head and looked up to see Carson standing on the other side of the counter of cantaloupes.

"What?" she asked in disbelief.

He grinned and then rubbed the back of his neck. "Sorry, it was just a joke. You were staring so intently at the produce I thought you were trying to see through it."

Esme chuckled when she realized she had been staring at the cantaloupes for a long time. "Sorry, lost in thought. What're you doing here? I thought you went to the co-op in Crater Lake?"

"I usually do, but I was in town visiting a friend and remembered I needed a few things." He walked around the produce counter to stand beside her. "I thought you usually shopped locally? I didn't even know you had a car."

"I don't. I took the bus down here." She picked up a melon and sniffed it, hoping this would be the end of the conversation, that he would get the hint to walk away. Instead he lingered.

Damn. Take a hint.

Carson whistled. "That's a pricey ticket to go grocery shopping."

Esme shrugged. "Didn't have a choice."

"The local co-op is a choice."

"The prices here are better?"

Carson smiled. "Why did you pose that in the form of a question? I doubt they're low enough to justify the price of a bus ticket."

"Are you really going to sit here and lecture me about my shopping habits?"

"No, but I can offer you a ride back to Crater Lake at the very least."

Say no.

Only she couldn't, because she really didn't want to lug all her groceries on the passenger bus back up to Crater Lake. And after this one excursion she knew she'd either have to invest in a car or just pluck up the courage to shop at the co-op, because she obviously couldn't avoid Carson even two towns away.

"Thanks. I appreciate that." She pushed her shopping cart away from the melons and Carson fell into step beside her.

"I haven't seen you around much," Carson remarked.

"I've been busy."

"I saw that Mrs. Fenolio is now one of your patients."

Esme sighed. "Are you going to start on me about stealing your patients again?"

"No. I'm not. Honestly, I'm glad that she's headed over to you. You seem to have more of a grasp of cardio-thoracic care."

Her heart skipped a beat.

Oh, God. Had he found out?

"Who told you that?"

"I saw it with my own eyes, Esme. Only someone with cardio-thoracic knowledge would be able to perform that procedure in that kind of situation. I think you've done that more than once or even a couple of times."

He was really persisting about the procedure. He was digging for information, information she didn't want to share. Information she wasn't going to share. It was in her past. She was here to start a new life. She wasn't that person any longer.

"I must have really impressed you."

"Well…yes." And he looked away quickly, rubbing the back of his neck again, as if he was embarrassed. As if he didn't want to give her a compliment.

"It was nothing. Now, about Mrs. Fenolio…"

"She's your patient now and you're the expert."

"I'm not. Not really."

Liar.

"Besides, she's only moved over her cardio care to me. How long has she had that murmur?"

"Do you really want to talk about this in a grocery store?" Carson asked as he picked up a loaf of bread and plunked it into her cart.

"Since when am I buying you groceries?" Esme teased.

"It's my fee for taking you back to Crater Lake. You can buy me my sandwiches for a week."

Esme chuckled. "I'm so disappointed."

"Why?"

"You're a sandwich man."

"What's wrong with liking sandwiches?" he asked.

"Nothing per se, but I'm a bit of a foodie."

Carson snorted. "Right, I forgot you're from Los Angeles."

"You don't have to be from LA to be a foodie. You can be from small towns, too. Not that I expect many people from Crater Lake to have many options."

"What're you talking about?" he asked.

"Oh, come on. Ray's is a fantastic Mom and Pop shop, but it's hardly gourmet."

"We have gourmet in Crater Lake," he said, sounding mildly insulted.

Esme looked skeptical. "Do you?"

"We do, but it's a bit of a secret."

"A secret?"

"Would you be interested in sampling a dinner there? I mean, since you're such a gourmand."

A zing traveled down her spine. Was he asking her out on a date? No. He couldn't be. She should say no, just on the off chance, but then again she couldn't resist a chance at a gourmet experience in Crater Lake.

It was better than sitting at home alone.

Don't do it.

"Okay...but as long as it's not up at the lodge." She didn't want too many people to see her with Carson. She wanted a low profile in town.

"No, it's not up at the lodge. It's been around longer than the lodge."

"Sure, then. Sounds intriguing."

"Good. So perhaps tonight?"

"Tonight?" she asked, trying not to let her voice hitch in her throat. "So soon?"

She thought maybe a day or two so she could get used to the idea.

"Is there something wrong with tonight? Do you have plans?"

Lie. Tell him you're busy.

Of course, if it was tonight she could get it done and out of the way.

"No. Tonight is fine. That's if you can get reservations to such an exclusive posh restaurant."

"Trust me. I can."

"Okay, then, it's a…" She paused because she was going to say *date*, but that was not what it was. At least she wasn't going to admit that was what it was. If she said it was a date, then it was and she couldn't have that. It was like eating a whole cake when no one saw you—the calories didn't count.

You know better than that. The calories do count.

And she might've just bitten off a little bit more than she could chew at the moment.

Carson couldn't believe what he'd just done, but before he could even think logically about what he was doing he was asking her out to a nonexistent restaurant. He was asking her over to his place, for dinner tonight. Carson couldn't help but think that he'd set himself up for failure and he didn't know why he'd asked her out.

Carson hadn't asked out anyone since Danielle.

He'd sworn off women when Danielle left and broke his heart.

He didn't want to get hurt again. It should be a simple matter staying away from Esme, but he couldn't.

He was drawn to her like a moth to a flame and he knew if he kept up this way he was going to get burnt.

Bad.

He was a masochist.

Perhaps she'd only said yes because she wanted to discover this great new restaurant in a very small town. Some hidden gem. Foodies liked to find hidden and new restaurants, especially places that were off the beaten trail, so to speak, and it was all innocent.

Yet the things she stirred deep down inside him were hardly innocent. And it scared him that she stirred desires that he'd buried long ago.

How would she feel when he picked her up and took her to his place, out in the woods? Not that he was that far out in the woods. He had an acre of wood lot and a nice cabin, which Luke had helped him build years ago, when Carson had thought he was building a home for him and Danielle.

There were neighbours within sight, but how would a city girl feel being brought out into the woods by a man she barely knew? He could be a serial killer for all she knew.

You're overthinking things again.

"You've gone positively pale," Esme remarked as they walked side by side through the store.

"What?" he asked.

"Are you okay?"

"I'm fine."

She frowned. "I don't think you are. You totally drifted off there. If it's about tonight, we can make it for another night."

"No, no, it's not that."

Yes, it is. You're setting yourself up for hurt.

"Are you sure?"

"Positive. I was just thinking about one of my files."

"Mrs. Fenolio?"

"Uh, yeah, sure."

Esme bit her lip. "We can talk about it tonight. I get that she's been at your family practice for some time. I understand it's hard to let go of some patients. Boy, do I ever." She mumbled the *Boy, do I ever* and he couldn't help but wonder why. Did she lose a patient that it still affected her so profoundly?

The loss of a patient was something that never sat right with Carson, but then, working in his father's practice, the patients they would lose were elderly. He wasn't a surgeon. Patients rarely died on his table.

When he thought about heading down that path to become a surgeon, he quickly changed his mind because he didn't want to just stitch them up and send them on their way. He wanted a connection with them. He wanted to be their primary caregiver.

It hurt when one of his patients died or became ill, but it wasn't the same as being responsible for someone's death and he couldn't help but wonder if Esme had experienced that.

"You lost a patient in LA?" he asked as they walked slowly down an aisle.

"Why would you ask me that?" She didn't look at him; she pretended to be studying the cans on the shelves.

"Because you're avoiding eye contact with me."

She shrugged and briefly glanced in his direction. "I'm not avoiding eye contact with you."

"You are too. I can tell when patients are lying to me."

She frowned. "I'm not your patient."

"Semantics."

Esme sighed. "I did lose a patient. It was hard, but

I moved on. You can't tell me that when you lost your first patient in your first year it didn't affect you?"

Esme was twisting the subject around back to him. It was a good evasive maneuver that he'd used many times to avoid uncomfortable questions.

Impressive.

"Well?" There was a small smile tugging at the corners of her lips.

"Okay, it affected me. Of course it would affect me. Anyone with any sense of compassion would feel that loss keenly."

"Exactly."

Carson decided he would drop the subject. For now, but he was still going to dig into her cardio-thoracic past. He was convinced that a family physician, just a family physician, wouldn't be able to perform such a procedure with such skill and precision.

She'd been so sure of herself.

So confident.

In that moment Esme had reminded him of a surgeon. A bit of her reminded him of Danielle. The drive, the ambition, and someone with that kind of passion wouldn't want to stay in such a place as Crater Lake.

They didn't talk much about anything else. They finished their grocery shopping and he drove the hour back to Crater Lake. Just chatting politely about nothing really. It was the most uncomfortable car ride Carson had ever taken in his life.

The whole way back to town he tried not to think about Danielle and how her leaving had left a hole in his heart. It had hurt, but he'd moved on. He'd built a solid practice with his father. He was safe and secure.

At least he'd thought his existence was safe and secure. He was comfortable. That was until Esme Petersen had set up shop in town and that had totally rocked the foundation of his safety net. He wasn't sure if he liked it.

Don't you?

He shook his head as he pulled up in front of her clinic.

"So what time will you be picking me up?" Esme asked.

"About seven?"

"Sure. That sounds great." She smiled; it was bright and cheerful. It warmed his heart, made him feel things he hadn't felt in a long time and that scared him.

Back out of the date.

He knew he was playing with fire, but he couldn't help himself. It was just an innocent dinner. He wanted to find out more about her, about her practice and maybe discuss some cases. Things that Luke never wanted to do, things he used to discuss with his father before his parents had upped and moved to Naples, Florida.

"Is there a dress code at this restaurant?" Esme asked, still not getting out of his car.

"No."

She glanced at him. "A gourmet restaurant and no dress code. I think I'm liking this place already."

Carson chuckled. "You'll like it. Trust me."

"And if I don't?" she asked.

"Then I owe you one."

Esme just grinned, but didn't say anything more as she opened the car door. "Pop the trunk for me and I'll see you at seven."

"Seven. I'll be waiting."

Esme climbed out and shut the door, collecting her groceries from the trunk and shutting it. She waved and then headed down the alley toward the back of her clinic.

Carson gripped the steering wheel and sat there for a few moments. What was he doing? He didn't really know. When Danielle had left him, when she'd crushed his heart, his hopes and dreams, he'd sworn he wouldn't let someone in again.

No dating, no nothing.

He was comfortable in his existence.

There were no surprises.

It was nice.

And it was also absolutely and utterly boring.

CHAPTER FIVE

ESME WANTED TO call and cancel the dinner date about three times before seven o'clock. The only problem was she didn't know Carson's phone number. She knew his office number, but the clinic was closed, so she was kind of stuck.

It's just as friends. Colleagues. Nothing more.

That was what she kept telling herself over and over again. The problem was, she wasn't sure if she was able to convince herself of that fact.

This was how it had started with Shane. A dinner with her mentor's son. As a favor to Eli, who hadn't been able to take his son out that night. It had been just a friendly dinner and then it had escalated from there. There was only one difference between Carson and Shane.

The simple fact was Carson Ralston made her nervous and no one made her nervous. Not Shane, not a difficult surgery. Just Carson.

Not even Eli Draven, the surgeon she idolized, made her nervous. He'd yelled and screamed at her before and she didn't care. The only reason she avoided Shane's father was because it reminded her of how she'd hurt Shane.

She was made of stronger mettle than to fold under the pressure of someone like Eli. Of course, Eli was someone else she'd disappointed.

Her father had always taught her to be strong. To stand up for herself and not let anyone walk all over her. Not that Carson was walking all over her. It was just that being around him made her nervous. He made her blood rush, her stomach zing and her body heat.

Carson made her weak in the knees. He made her think of romance and she wasn't a romance type of girl. Love only led to heartache. The only time she'd come close to anything romantic was when she'd almost married Shane on Valentine's Day, and look where that had got her.

Yet, being around Carson made her nervous, made her irrational.

There were times she could feel the heat in her cheeks from blushing and Esme had never blushed in someone's presence before.

Not since she was in the seventh grade and had that crush on Matthew Fenwick.

You do not have a crush on Dr. Ralston.

That was what she kept trying to tell herself over and over again. She didn't have a crush on Carson. She couldn't have a crush on him, she just couldn't, because she didn't deserve it. Men like Carson needed a wife and Esme wasn't wife material. Something that had become quite clear to her when she'd picked up the voluminous skirt of her designer wedding dress and climbed out of the bathroom window of the church, running in the opposite direction to Shane.

He'd demanded so much of her. He'd wanted her by his side constantly, which had taken her away from surgery. She'd forgotten about why she'd become a surgeon. She'd realized all of this when she'd frozen during surgery. How dating Shane had made her off her game.

How could she be the best cardio-thoracic surgeon if she was a society wife and mother? With Shane she couldn't. She couldn't be herself. So Esme had run. *I don't know who you are anymore. I didn't raise a daughter who runs.*

Her father's voice was still so clear in her mind.

She didn't know who she was. Not anymore.

A textbook procedure on a patient and she'd frozen. Not knowing what to do next.

Lost.

And then it had all come back in a rush and despite her best efforts she hadn't been able to save the patient. It hadn't mattered that it hadn't been her fault, that she had done everything she could. All she'd been able to see was her failure in that moment.

That was when she'd walked away from surgery. She was done. Broken. From there things had spiraled and it had led to the collapse of her plans for happy ever after with Shane. If only she could have known her own heart sooner.

That was why she had left Los Angeles. To find herself again. Though that was easier said than done, because her guilty conscience was attacking her at every angle.

She'd run away.

She'd disappointed her father.

Still, there had been no choice in the matter. Here she could live in peace. Here she didn't have to run.

When it came to matters of the heart though, that

was where she was weak. Maybe she should run now? Go somewhere else until Carson left. Then she wouldn't have to go out to dinner with him and then she wouldn't have to feel so nervous around him.

Carson's SUV pulled up in front of her building. He honked the horn a couple of times. Esme sighed and grabbed her purse.

No turning back now. She just hoped she was dressed okay. She didn't want to stick out like a sore thumb. She'd opted for casual classy. A nice pair of jeans, boots and a black sweater that was off the shoulders. Also accessories.

So no matter where he took her, she'd blend in and that was what it was all about. She just wanted to blend in. She didn't want to stand out.

She didn't want to be extraordinary, because she wasn't. Not anymore anyway.

When she walked over to the car Carson got out and held open the door for her.

"You didn't have to get out," she said.

"My mother taught me good manners." Once she was in the car he shut the door and then slid back into the driver's seat, buckling up before he pulled away. "So this place we're going, it's out in the country. I didn't want to freak you out or anything."

"Why would I freak out?" she asked.

"You know, a man you barely know is taking you out into the wilderness."

Esme chuckled. "I assumed it was out of town."

"You did?"

"Main Street, or rather the town of Crater Lake, isn't that huge. The only eating establishments within the major downtown core are Ray's, Little Mamma's Bakery and Main Street Deli…which has been closed for repairs for a seemingly long time."

"Twenty years," Carson responded.

"That's a shame. I enjoy a good sandwich." She tried not to laugh. It was so easy to tease him. All the trepidation she'd been feeling seemed to melt away and that was what scared her. It was so easy to be around him.

"What? I thought you had an issue with sandwiches. I mean, that's why I'm taking you to this exclusive spot. You seemed to have a problem with my sandwiches when we were shopping today."

"I like traditional deli sandwiches within moderation. Somehow, though, I think that you're taking bologna sandwiches to work. Two pieces of white bread, mustard, an imitation cheese slice and a piece of bologna. Just like Mom used to pack in school lunches."

"All smooshed down and everything?" Carson asked.

Esme smiled. "Yes, with the crusts cut off."

He shook his head. "You think you know me so well. I'll have you know it's not just bologna in my repertoire. I also enjoy a good salami."

She couldn't help but break out laughing at that and when he realized what he'd said a blush crept up his cheeks and he shot her an exasperated look.

"That's not what I meant at all and you know it."

"Do I? I barely know you," she said. "You could be an axe murderer or something. A doctor who injects his patients with a live virus just so he can test his maniacal cures on them."

"Hardly."

"Whatever you say, Dr. Moreau." Then she laughed.

"Fine, then. Believe what you want." He winked and turned down a gravel drive. She glanced out the window as she saw a beautiful log home in a clearing, built into the side of a foothill.

"What is this place?" she asked.

"The exclusive restaurant. Also known as my house."

Her heart beat a bit faster. *His house?* This was dangerous.

"Your house?" she asked, the words barely getting out.

"I'm sorry for tricking you. I guess I should've explained that it was my place I was taking you to."

"Yeah, you should've."

"Would you have come?"

"No," she said. "I don't think so." And it was true. She wouldn't have. Having dinner with him was temptation enough. She'd thought at least other people would be around. Now they'd be alone, out in the woods in his gorgeous cabin. Suddenly, she was very nervous again. *Dammit.*

It was all too seductive for her liking.

"Sorry, but I wanted to prove to you that I'm not just a sandwich guy. Even though I'm not from LA and I don't have exposure to some of the best restaurants in America, I do have experience of some gastronomical delights."

"That remains to be seen."

"You don't believe me?" he asked in mild outrage.

"My expectations were set high," she teased. "You have a lot to live up to, Dr. Ralston."

Carson parked his car. "You can call me Carson. We're not on duty."

Blood rushed to her cheeks and she turned her head away briefly, hoping he wouldn't notice how he was affecting her physically.

Think about something else.

"Okay. You can call me Esme. I mean, no one else is around so no one has to know we've formed this sort of ceasefire."

"Right."

They got out of the car and she followed him up the steps to the front porch. She stopped to take in the breathtaking sight. From the front porch she could see Crater Lake, nestled in the foothills, like in a little valley. The mountains in Glacier National Park rising up to protect the town, as if it were this little sheltered place. Untouched and hidden.

"Wow," she whispered.

"I know. When I have time I like to sit out here at night. It's also beautiful in the morning with the sun rising."

Lucky.

If this was her place she'd do the exact same thing.

Esme walked over to the railing and leaned over, taking in her surroundings. She spotted another house, down the hill in the trees. It looked dark, but lived in. "Whose house is that?"

Carson came up beside her and she was suddenly aware of how close he actually was. His hand so close to her on the wooden railing, they were almost touching. She could smell his cologne. It was subtle, masculine and very woodsy. It made her tremble. It made her weak in the knees.

It turned her on.

So she moved an inch away, trying to put distance between them.

"That's my childhood home. Or rather my parents' house. They come back and visit from time to time. That's where they stay. This land is my family's land. With me nearby I can keep an eye on my parents' house."

"Where are they now?"

"Naples, Florida. They have a condo that backs out onto a golf course. They love it there."

"And I hear you have a brother, right?"

Carson nodded. "Yes. I do."

"Does he live there or here with you?"

"No, he lives up the mountain in a shack."

Esme rolled her eyes. "Are you having me on? He doesn't live in a shack."

"Yes, he does."

"I thought you said he was a doctor."

"He is, but he lives in a shack up the mountain. He's a bit of a mountain man. He doesn't practice traditional medicine. He was an army medic for years in Special Ops and then after he was discharged he liked living in the rough so much he built a shanty out in the woods. He takes surveyors out; he's a first responder. He teaches people how to survive in the hostile environment of a mountain. He will do emergency surgery."

"Emergency surgery in the woods?"

"Sometimes there's no choice."

Esme cringed inwardly at the thought of emergency surgery out in the forest. Hardly ideal, but if you were an ex-army man living rough in a remote community, then it made sense.

"Wow. All the power to him." She moved away from

him. "So are you going to let me inside or are we going to stand here all night?"

Carson grinned and unlocked the front door, stepping aside. "After you."

She tried not to gasp when she stepped inside his house. She was expecting rustic, but on a smaller scale. She was not prepared for the high roof, exposed wooden beams and the massive stone fireplace that dominated the northern wall. All around them were windows, which offered a three-sixty view of the mountains, the town and a lake that seemed to be sunk in, like a hollow. Even in the evening sunlight, you could see its brilliant coral and aquamarine colors. In the center the blue darkened, like a deep hole.

She'd seen the Great Blue Hole in Belize; this wasn't as big, but it was still impressive given the setting. She moved toward the far window to get a better look at the lake. There was no wind outside so the mountains were perfectly reflected in the water. Like a mirror. It was the most beautiful thing she'd ever seen.

Carson came up behind her; she could feel the heat of his body against her back. It made her uncomfortable and she remembered his arm around her when he'd tried to comfort her on the trip up the mountain to the mill. She shifted away, trying to put some distance between the two of them.

Distance was safe.

"What's the name of the lake?"

"That's Crater Lake, what the town was named after."

"I expected something different for Crater Lake."

"Different?"

"Something bigger perhaps." He smiled at her, that smile that made her melt just a little bit. This was why Carson was dangerous.

"I think it's pretty substantial." Carson raked his hand through his hair and then crossed his arms. When he had the blinds in his office windows open, she watched him dictating charts, just like that. His arms crossed, head bent and usually pacing back and forth.

There was something calming about it. Soothing. It made her feel at ease.

She couldn't think about him like that.

"Why is it so blue?" Esme asked, trying not to think about the fact she was standing in Carson's home, that he made her calm and yet nervous at the same time. She couldn't think about him this way. She didn't want to.

This was not what she was here for.

"Mineral water off the glacier in the mountains. When the water is blue like that, it's from the glaciers. If it's more clear, more like a normal lake, it's spring fed." He moved past her to the south end of the house and pointed. "That's Mitchum Lake—see the difference. It's spring fed."

"I think these are better views than where that new resort community was built on the other side of town. I'm surprised that no one made you an offer on this land."

"Who says they didn't?" Carson grinned. "Would you like some wine?"

Esme nodded as he moved past her to the kitchen.

"I'm sure it was a lot of money they must've offered. Most people wouldn't turn that down."

"I'm not most people." He winked and set down two wine glasses on the counter. "Red okay?"

"Perfect." She dropped her purse on an end table. "So what do you plan to cook for me tonight?"

"Bison."

What? "Did I just hear you correctly? Did you say bison?"

"I could cook you elk if you'd prefer?"

"Bison is fine. I have to say I'm disappointed."

Carson cocked an eyebrow and then started to get food ready for dinner. "Why?"

"Isn't Montana famous for beefsteak?"

He flexed and made pointed glances at his biceps, which made her laugh out loud. She couldn't remember the last time she'd laughed like that. It was so easy to laugh with Carson. When the giggles stopped she followed him out onto his deck, which overlooked the lake. He had a stainless-steel barbecue there, where he was grilling the bison steaks.

Esme wandered over to the side and leaned over the railing. She could see the construction off in the distance where the new Draven resort and spa were going to go up. They were going to be an eyesore.

At least that was Esme's opinion.

"What're you thinking about?" Carson asked.

"Pardon?"

Carson glanced over his shoulder at her. "I asked you what you were thinking about. You were staring off into space. You do that a lot."

She couldn't tell him why she had been doing that a lot lately and he was right, she had been drifting off. It was nice and quiet. It was easy enough to do around here.

"I was relaxing and enjoying the view."

"Easy to do," Carson said as he turned back to the

grill and flipped the meat. "I've thought about putting a hot tub out here."

"That would be nice. Especially in the winter, I bet."

"Have you ever experienced winter?" Carson asked.

"Yes, I wasn't born and raised in California. I'm from Ohio."

"So you're used to bitter winters."

Esme nodded. "Yeah, but it's been a long time since I experienced one. I'm honestly not looking forward to it."

He laughed. "I don't doubt it."

"Can I help?"

"You can grab the cobs of corn in the fridge, then I can grill them here on the barbecue."

"Sure thing." Esme set her wine glass down on the patio table and headed inside. She found the shucked corn in the fridge and brought it back to Carson, who threw it on the grill. "Why don't we eat outside?"

"Sure. We can do that."

Esme headed back inside and found plates and cutlery. She brought everything outside and set it all out. Just in time for the meat and corn to be done.

They sat down together.

"I hope you like it. My brother says I'm the best at grilling bison."

"Well, since I have nothing to compare it to." Esme took a bite. It was so tender and absolutely delicious. She'd tried lots of different food before, but never bison.

"What do you think?" Carson asked.

"It's fantastic."

"See, I told you it was the best place in town."

"You were right. Great view, too."

"I always thought so. It's why I built my house here."

Esme was stunned. "You built this house?"

"I did. I like working with my hands. I like building things. I didn't draw up the plans, but I did a lot of the work myself. Luke and my father helped, too."

"That's amazing. Most doctors I know just participate in golf or attend parties at their club."

"Those are surgeons. I can't see a surgeon risking injuring their hands by doing work like this. Well, at least not any surgeons I know."

"I thought you didn't know any surgeons?"

Carson sighed. "Well, I do have to refer my patients who need work to surgeons. Thankfully, most of those surgeons are in Missoula."

"You don't like surgeons very much, do you?"

"Who said that? I have no problems with surgeons. There are some general practitioners I know who are just as goofy as the ones in Missoula."

Esme laughed. "So I take it you don't have many friends?"

"I'm a bit of a loner. I prefer it that way."

"Me, too." And she did, to some extent, but suddenly the idea of going back to her apartment above her clinic made her sad. She had a hard time falling asleep in the quiet.

She wanted to be alone, she didn't deserve happiness, but still. It sucked. And sitting here with Carson made her forget for just a moment that she was lonely. It was amazing being here with him and just talking.

Which was a dangerous thing indeed.

Carson smiled at her; when he smiled like that there was a dimple in his cheek. It was so sexy. She was a sucker for dimples on a man. There were a lot of enticing qualities about Carson. He was so different from

Shane. So down to earth, but she could tell he wasn't the type of guy to be pushed around by anyone.

She was definitely treading on dangerous ground here.

"So Mrs. Fenolio is quite stubborn."

Carson chuckled under his breath. "I thought you didn't want to talk about Mrs. Fenolio?"

"I didn't want to talk about her in the store, but I'm willing to discuss her file with her former physician in this private setting."

She was trying in vain to turn the conversation around. If they talked about work she wouldn't think about how good he looked in the button-down flannel shirt he was wearing, the tight starched jeans and the cowboy boots. Or the fact that he was a fantastic cook.

If they talked about the patient, she wouldn't stare at his slim hips or those muscular forearms or his smiling face with the devious sparkle in his eyes. A sparkle that was promising lots of very bad things that she really wanted to indulge in.

Damn.

He nodded and poured the wine. "You have knowledge in cardio-thoracic surgery."

"A bit."

He looked at her. "Oh, we're going to play this game again."

"I'm not playing any games, Dr. Ralston."

"Carson."

She glared at him. "Carson, then."

"Better."

She sighed. "Okay, I spent some time in a hospital before I decided to open a family practice and that's all you need to know about the matter."

* * *

Carson wanted to press her further, because he felt as if here she was opening up more, but then he didn't want to scare her away either. She might be the competition, but maybe, just maybe, if they were on good terms they could work together and do something more. The town was expanding and it might be nice to have a larger practice. Something his father had never dreamed of.

If it's not broken you don't fix it. That was his father's mantra when it came to business. Thankfully not when it came to medicine.

The Ralston family practice had been the way it was since the town was founded. It was sufficient and efficient.

If a patient required any other kind of care that the practice didn't offer, the hospital was only an hour away. That was the reason why they had air ambulance up in this part of Montana.

The family practice was solid.

It didn't need to be changed and just thinking about that change scared him. He shouldn't be thinking about changing it. What would change do? It could potentially destroy everything his family had built. Did he really want to cause the demise of the Ralston family practice?

He wasn't the one who was going to end that legacy.

Carson wasn't that person. Even if he wanted more, he wasn't going to change a thing.

He turned around and put a stopper in the wine, setting it on the far counter, his back to Esme so she couldn't see him. He didn't want to be thinking about Danielle. Not here, not now. Also it got his mind off the fact Esme was in his home and that his bedroom was just ten feet away. She was so damn sexy and he had to keep reminding himself she was off-limits. He refused to get hurt again.

He had to stop staring at the curve of her neck, her red lips and her bare shoulders.

"I spent some time as a surgical intern, as well," Carson said casually as he handed her the glass of wine.

"Did you?"

"I did. For about three months and I realized that surgery is not my thing."

"Not your thing?" she asked. "Why?"

"I want to save lives."

Her brow furrowed. "You don't think surgeons save lives? They're all about saving lives. They endure grueling training, long hours and sometimes life-threatening situations so they *can* save a life."

There was a fire in her eyes as she passionately defended surgery.

Not a surgeon, my foot.

"How long were you a surgical intern?"

"Ah, a year, and then I decided to open a practice in Los Angeles."

"Huh, I thought you might've gone all the way."

Esme shot him that flinty glare again, the one he was quickly learning to fear. It was the look she seemed to give when someone had pushed her too far. "Why would you assume that?"

"Because you talked so passionately about surgery. Only surgeons talk with such passion and fire about surgery, because those who are meant to be surgeons are married to it. It's their first love."

The glare softened and she smiled. "I just respect them. That's all."

He nodded. "I respect them, too, and I quickly learned in my few months that I was not a surgeon and that was probably for the best for all patients."

She laughed at his joke, the tension melting away. "Well, I tried a new prescription regimen on Mrs. Fenolio, but darned if I can get her to take it."

Carson frowned. "A new prescription regimen? Why?"

"What she was taking for her condition was not working anymore."

"Digoxin wasn't working anymore? Physicians have been using digoxin since the pioneer days."

"Yes, and it did work fine. In Mrs. Fenolio's case it doesn't apply any longer. She's suffering from ventricular tachycardia. In Mrs. Fenolio's case amiodarone works substantially better."

He frowned again. "That's horrible. I'm sorry she's deteriorated. My father was treating her for a decade."

"And he did fantastic. Mrs. Fenolio's disease is progressing rapidly. I've actually added her to the transplant list."

"You...you did what?" Carson was baffled. For a decade his father had treated Mrs. Fenolio and there had been no issues. She had survived and now suddenly Esme was standing here in his kitchen saying that Mrs. Fenolio required a heart transplant. He was having a hard time believing it. Probably because Mrs. Fenolio used to babysit him and Luke. Especially given the fact Esme had only completed her intern year, something she'd just told him. He could believe that a physician who had one year of surgical training could complete the procedure she'd performed up at the mill, but changing Mrs. Fenolio's treatment plan completely and telling the woman she needed a heart transplant? That wasn't someone who did just a year as an intern. It firmed his belief Esme was a surgeon.

"What're you basing your opinion on?" he asked.

"On the tests I ran in my clinic and the fact she wore a Holter monitor for twenty-four hours."

"You admitted yourself that you're not a cardio-thoracic specialist. How can you diagnose someone? How can you make that call to put her on the transplant list? You can't. Only a surgeon can do that."

Her eyes widened for a moment as if he'd caught her in a lie and she was trying to think up an excuse.

"Well?" Carson asked impatiently. "Someone who only completed one year of internship of surgery can't diagnose that condition. They wouldn't know and a general practitioner can't put a patient on the transplant waiting list without a surgeon's assessment. Admit you're a surgeon, Dr. Petersen."

"You've lost your mind." She put down her wine glass and grabbed her purse. "I think I'm going to head for home."

Carson stood in front of her, blocking her path. "You're a surgeon, Esme. You have an incredible talent. I've never seen anyone drain a cardiac tamponade or recognize a Beck's Triad that quickly in that kind of situation. I just don't know why you're trying to hide it from me."

She stared up at him. Those blue eyes, so wide. She was afraid to admit it, but why? Why should she be so afraid to admit that she had a gift? Yeah, maybe he didn't want the life of a surgeon. Maybe he'd left something he'd always dreamed about to uphold a family tradition, but why would she throw something extraordinary away?

"I…I don't know what to…"

He gripped her shoulders. "You can tell me. You have skill, Esme. Amazing talent."

"Carson, I don't know you and you don't know me. I shouldn't be having this conversation with you."

"You can trust me."

"Can I?"

"Yes," he whispered as he reached out and brushed back her hair. It was so soft and he fought the urge to kiss her, because that was what he wanted to do. He wanted to kiss her. Badly. "Tell me. You can tell me."

"You might think less of me."

"Doubtful."

Esme smiled, but in a sad way that made his soul ache a bit. "So sure of yourself. I had confidence like that once."

"You still do."

"No, I don't."

"Yes, you do. That was a confident doctor I saw up on that mountain."

She was going to say something else when his door opened and Luke came barging in.

"Carson, I've been looking all over for you." Then he saw Esme. "Sorry, I didn't realize you had company."

Esme pushed out of his embrace. "I was just heading back to town."

"Good, you both need to head back to town," Luke

said. He sounded a bit winded. "I thought you two would be down at the clinic."

"What's going on, Luke?" Carson asked.

"I brought a surveyor down off the mountain. His appendix is going to blow. There's no time to take him to the hospital."

CHAPTER SIX

EVEN IF SHE wanted to hide the fact that she was a surgeon from Carson now, there was no way she could. Not when there was a life on the line.

With this surveyor who was in Carson's exam room in agony, she wasn't going to let the man die from a ruptured appendix because she had something to hide.

Because she was scared.

She was going to operate on him. She might not practice as a surgeon now, but she was a surgeon. Lives were in her hands.

This man's life was in her hands. Luke was examining the surveyor while Carson began to strip off his clothes in the other room. She knew she shouldn't watch, but she couldn't help it. He saw her watching him and her cheeks bloomed with heat as his intense gaze burned into her soul. He pulled out a pair of scrubs and tossed them to her.

"You're not going to want to get your clothes dirty," Carson said. "They look too...nice to get ruined."

"Thanks."

He nodded and turned his back to her as he finished changing. Esme snuck into his office and quickly peeled off her clothes and pulled on the men's scrubs, pulling the drawstring as tight as she could, but they were still large.

As she pulled on her shirt Carson came bursting in, pausing in the doorway. He looked away quickly, rubbing the back of his neck in that awkward way he always did.

"I'm sorry. I thought you were finished."

"It's okay. I'm done. I'm impressed you keep scrubs on hand."

"My father always insisted. I guess in case of emergencies like this."

"I thought he wasn't a surgeon," Esme teased.

Carson smiled. "I never said that. You look nervous. You okay?"

"I'm okay. It's just…"

"It's nothing. You can do this."

"It's a simple surgery."

"Exactly. It'll be easy."

Easy. Right. Though she wasn't sure. The last surgery she'd done was routine. It had been easy and she'd frozen.

"I'll see you in there. Have you performed an appendectomy before?" she asked.

"Once, in the few months I was an intern."

"How about your brother?" she asked.

"He's performed several emergency procedures in extreme situations. He was an army medic. He's a surgeon, but he's not staying. He left the rest of the surveyors up on the mountain."

Esme nodded. "Oh. Well, you'll have to handle the anesthesia."

"Of course."

Esme let him change and entered the exam room

where Luke was pulling down supplies to perform the surgery in this place. The patient had been given morphine and was basically in and out of consciousness.

"Have you performed surgery before, Dr. Petersen?" Luke asked.

"Yes. Many times."

Luke nodded. "Good, I need to get back up the mountain. Carson said you were a surgeon."

"I was. I am." She cursed under her breath as she stumbled over her words. "I've performed more appendectomies than I care to admit."

Luke grinned and nodded. "Fair enough, Dr. Petersen."

She made her way over to the sink and scrubbed the best she could given the situation. Four-minute scrub. Could she even remember the words to the song she sang when she scrubbed? And then it came back to her. She scrubbed and it felt weird to be scrubbing for surgery again, but also it felt good. "Has he been given any antibiotic?"

"Doing that now, Dr. Petersen," Carson said as he was setting up an IV. Carson's brother had left. It was just the two of them here. Alone.

She might have done a ton of appendectomies and emergency appendectomies, but she'd never done one outside of the OR and not in these conditions. Though she was pretty positive if Luke Ralston was a former army medic, he'd probably seen worse. And right now she really didn't need to see worse.

There were no scrub nurses so Esme scurried to lay out the surgical instruments and the supplies she'd need.

"He's under," Carson said over his shoulder as he intubated the man. "I can assist you if you need."

"No, just manage his airway."

Carson nodded. "I'm here if you need me, but you got this."

Esme took a deep breath and palpated the patient's abdomen.

You can do it. You're a surgeon. This guy won't die.

This was just an appendectomy. This was not an open heart. Appendectomies were routine. She could do this.

You used to be able to do open hearts, too.

She *had* to do this. Help was too far away for this man. He wouldn't survive unless she did this. Esme took another deep calming breath, took the ten blade in hand and made the incision over McBurney's point. Once she was cutting down through the layers, everything fell into place. She remembered everything. It was routine. It was easy.

Her hands didn't shake.

Carson watched and then began to assist her while managing the man's airway. As if reading her thoughts he knew what instruments to hand her. The only sound was the rhythmic beat of the manual ventilator.

She found her rhythm as a surgeon again, even though it had been months since she held a scalpel. She'd forgotten what a high it was. How much she loved it. Not that she deserved to love something so much.

Still, it was a thrill. It was amazing.

All too soon she was pulling on the purse strings and inverting the stump into the cecum and closing him up.

"Excellent work, Dr. Petersen," Carson remarked.

"Thank you, Dr. Ralston." She glanced up at him while he continued to manually ventilate the patient. "Has an ambulance been called to take him to the hospital? You may be set up to do emergency surgery, but you're not set up for post-op care. He's going to need a course of antibiotics."

"Yes," Carson said. "I called from my office before we started."

Esme finished stitching and heard the sirens coming closer toward them.

"Speak of the devil," Carson muttered. "Dr. Petersen, can you take over the ventilation and I'll let the paramedics in as I know the surveyor and can give them the information they need."

"Of course." Esme pulled off her gloves, throwing them into the receptacle and putting on a fresh pair. She took over the manual ventilation since she was finished stitching, cleaned the wound and applied the pressure dressing. Carson returned quickly.

"I didn't expect to be doing that again," Esme said.

"You did an amazing job." Then he smiled at her in a way that made her heart melt. "I knew you could."

Why did he have so much faith in her?

She cleared her throat and looked away. "Your clinic was very well prepared for surgery."

"My father and Luke were always insistent on being prepared for any situation. Especially up here in the mountains," Carson said. "First time it has happened under my watch, though."

"Smart move, given the hospital is more than an hour away. This man didn't have an hour in him."

"Accidents and emergencies up here can happen when you least expect it," Carson said, peeling off his gloves. "You did well."

"Thank you." And she blushed again, their gazes locked across the room. She wanted to say more, but couldn't. She just couldn't. She had to keep her distance from Carson.

"There's no need to thank me," Carson said. "I'm just speaking the truth."

"Well, you don't need to say I did well. There's no need. I wasn't going to let him die. I did what needed to be done."

"I know that, but—"

Their conversation ended abruptly as the paramedics entered the exam room. Esme let them take over as they brought in their equipment. In a matter of minutes the paramedics had the surveyor loaded up, leaving Carson and Esme to clean up the clinic. She didn't know what Carson was going to say to her there, but it didn't matter.

Whatever it was, she didn't need to hear it.

They worked side by side in silence. She knew she couldn't really hide who she was. Not after this moment. She admitted it, but she didn't want to tell him why. She didn't want to get into it and she hated that her past was sneaking into her present life.

"So…" He trailed off.

"I was a surgeon in Los Angeles. More than an intern."

Carson smiled. "I figured that."

She laughed uneasily. "I'm not a surgeon anymore."

He stopped his cleaning. "Why?"

Because I froze during a procedure and a patient died on my table. I lost my confidence. I lost myself.

"I wanted a quiet life." Then she laughed at the absurdity of that and he joined in. "I thought Crater Lake would be quiet."

"Well, it usually is. Come to think of it, it was until you came to town."

"Thanks for that." She grinned.

He winked. "Any time."

"I hope it calms down," she said offhandedly.

"With all these new people coming to town I doubt that very much. In fact I can see a hospital being built here."

"You say that like it's a bad thing."

Carson sighed. "No, it's not a bad thing. It's just... change."

"You don't like change, do you?" Esme asked.

"No, I don't. Not really."

"Why?"

Carson didn't say anything. He didn't even look at her and she realized that she must have touched a nerve. Something he was obviously not comfortable talking about. Why didn't he like change? Something had hurt him.

It's not your business.

And it wasn't. Yet he had pushed and pressed her about being a surgeon. Maybe it was tit for tat.

"Change can be good. I mean, I changed..." She trailed off. A lot had changed in her life, but then again maybe it hadn't. She had run away from her career and when she was holding that scalpel it felt so damn good. She felt as if she was at home and for that one brief moment she regretted the fact that she'd left the hospital. That she'd left surgery.

Esme zoned out and Carson couldn't help but wonder what she was thinking. He'd known she was a surgeon, even though she'd denied it. He'd known it the moment she'd stuck that needle into that patient's chest and drained fluid.

She had a gift. Such a tremendous gift.

And he couldn't help but wonder why she would want to give that up.

What is it to you?

It really wasn't his business at all. They were just neighbors, both doctors. Heck, they weren't even friends and even if they were friends it still wouldn't be his business. So why did he care so much?

"Did the change make a difference?" he asked.

"What change?"

"Moving here from LA. You said you changed."

She shrugged. "I think it did…"

"You don't sound certain."

"I haven't been here long enough, but, as they say, a change will do you good." She continued to clean up his exam room as he mulled over her words.

A change will do you good?

He wasn't sure he believed that. Why change something that worked? It was a dangerous thing to do, to ruin one's safety net. He'd tried to once. Tried to make a change in his life and look how that had turned out.

It had left him with a shattered heart, but he'd put away all those feelings in a box. Locked them away because taking over his father's practice had been the right thing to do. It was safe and comfortable. Packing up and moving out of state. Changing professions.

Throwing away a career. One that Carson knew she would've studied long and hard for. Surgeons competed. It was a shark tank and only the fittest survived.

Why would she give that up?

It's not your concern.

Then he realized it wasn't so much that he cared, but he was angry that such a talented surgeon was throwing away her gift. She could be using that education to save lives.

You save lives.

Only not in the same way. He saved people's lives, but not in the same way that she could save lives.

It was a waste and he wanted to tell her that. Berate her. Only he couldn't. That wasn't his place, but he just didn't understand how someone could walk away from talent like that.

One day soon she'd decide that a general practice in a small town in Montana wasn't surgery. She'd close her practice, his former patients would come back and she would go back to the exciting life of a surgical practice.

Just as Danielle had left.

Surgeons wanted more. They needed more.

More than he could offer and he had to distance himself now. He could handle this.

He didn't want to handle this.

He didn't want to be her friend.

He didn't want to be… Carson couldn't even finish that thought, because that thought was dangerous and out of the question.

"Are you okay?" she asked as she tossed the rest of the drapes into the receptacle.

"Fine," he snapped and then he cursed under his breath. "Just tired."

"It's been a long day."

"It has." He couldn't even look at her. Carson just had to get away from her. "Why don't you head home for the night? Like you said, it's been a long day."

"Are you sure you don't want me to stay and help you clean up?"

"Yeah, I'm sure. Just...go."

"Okay." Esme walked out of the room. "Should I leave the scrubs in your office?"

"Yeah, that's fine." Carson could barely look at her, because if he looked at her he might start lecturing her that she was throwing away all that talent that could be used for saving lives.

She nodded. "Okay. Good night, Dr. Ralston."

Carson just nodded as she left the exam room.

He had to keep away from Esme.

If he kept away from her his heart would be safe. If he kept away from her, maybe, just maybe, she'd realize the folly of her mistake and return to surgery where she belonged.

CHAPTER SEVEN

ESME SAW CARSON across the street, walking to his clinic with a cup of coffee, from where she was outside picking up the papers off the front step of her clinic. She hadn't seen him since the night of the emergency appendectomy three weeks ago.

If she saw him, he seemed to turn in the other direction and it was clear that he was avoiding her, which shouldn't bother her, but it did and she was mad at herself that his avoidance bothered her.

This was what she wanted. She wanted to keep her distance from him. She wasn't here to make friends. She wasn't here to find love. She was here to practice medicine.

When she first came to Crater Lake all she wanted was solitude. She wanted her practice and to be alone. She didn't need anyone. She didn't want anyone. That was why she'd left Shane, right, because she didn't want to be tied down to anyone.

She didn't want to chip away pieces of herself to suit someone else. Romance and love weren't for her. She'd proven that to the universe many times. Love only brought pain. Love made her forget who she was. It changed her.

And then she laughed at that thought. Three weeks ago she was telling Carson that change could be good. Yet she was not willing to change herself.

You've done that before, remember?

That was why it was good that he was avoiding her.

It was good, so why did it tick her off so much?

Probably because his change after the emergency appendectomy didn't make sense. One moment they were becoming friends. One minute his arms were on her and he was telling her that it was okay if she told him that she was a surgeon, asking her to open up, and now he'd closed her out.

She'd caught him watching her a few times during the surgery and she thought he'd looked impressed or awed. Maybe almost validated in his assessment of her.

Then when they'd been cleaning up, when she'd admitted that she was a surgeon, things had changed. Carson hadn't even been able to look her in the eye. As if he was disgusted with her, as if she was the worst person ever.

So what was his problem? He'd told her it would be okay if she divulged her secret. He'd lied to her. It clearly wasn't okay with him, but he was avoiding her now. She was tired of being ostracized. He had no right to judge her.

Doesn't he?

Esme ignored the voice in her head. Her grip around the flyers tightened and she marched across the road and blocked Carson's path to his clinic.

Carson stopped in midstep, surprised to see her standing there, and she knew by the way his eyes started darting around he was looking for a way to escape, but there was no way to escape. She had him trapped.

"Dr. Petersen," he said.

"Morning, Dr. Ralston. Long time no see."

He rubbed the back of his neck, in that way that he always seemed to do when he seemed to be uncomfortable. She usually found it sexy, but today it annoyed her.

"How can I help you today?"

You could tell me why you're being such a jerk. Only she didn't say out loud what she wanted to say.

Instead she asked, "How is the surveyor? You never updated me after the surgery. I was just wondering how he was doing."

"Mr. Tyner, the surveyor, he's fine. He spent a week in the hospital on IV antibiotics, but other than that he made it through fine. Once he recovers fully in about three more weeks he'll be back to work."

"And the others? Did Luke get them down off the mountain?"

"Yes. He did."

Esme nodded. "Thank you. I was…concerned. I figured the way you were avoiding me that perhaps he didn't make it. That you blamed me for his death, but he made it so…why are you avoiding me?"

"I'm not avoiding you, Esme. I've been busy."

"Busy."

"Yeah."

Awkward tension fell between them. He couldn't look her in the eyes. Something she was used to after she'd frozen during that surgery. Other surgeons had avoided her. They'd avoided working with her; her name had disappeared from the OR board numerous times. It was the same look on her father's face when she'd run out on Shane.

No one trusted her. She didn't trust herself either.

She was used to it, but she was getting tired of it.

Just turn around and walk away. Let him ignore you. It doesn't matter.

Only it did matter. It annoyed her. She didn't deserve this.

Don't you?

"Well, I'll let you get back to your busy day." Esme turned around to head back to her clinic, dumping the flyers into a recycling bin.

"Esme, wait up."

She glanced round to see Carson heading toward her. *Just ignore him.*

Only she couldn't. Even though she kept reminding herself over and over again that she didn't need anyone. That she was here in Crater Lake to just find herself again. She was lonely. She hadn't realized how much she enjoyed Carson's company until he was no longer talking to her.

So she waited for Carson, because, even though she didn't deserve to have friendship or companionship, she was lonely and she couldn't help herself. She couldn't help herself and that made her weak.

She was so weak. Especially when it came to him.

"I'm...not ignoring you. I mean I was, but...I'm sorry," Carson said. "It got intense in there and...look, I'm not used to intense situations."

"Fair enough."

"I should've told you about Mr. Tyner's recovery earlier. For that I'm sorry." And he smiled at her, those blue eyes of his twinkling.

Esme nodded. "Yeah, you should've. I mean, I may have been a surgeon and done quite a few appendectomies in my past, but that was the first time in a long time I've performed one in that kind of situation and not known the outcome. I was worried."

"I bet you were. I'm sorry."

"Thanks for telling me. I'm sorry if I attacked you there. Especially on a Sunday morning."

"You had every right to. I should've known better, but...well, it was my first time ever. I did a few months of a surgical internship, but I never did perform an appendectomy on my own."

"You never did a solo surgery?"

Carson shrugged. "What can I say? I wasn't a surgeon. I'm not a surgeon."

"I would ask you if you were fired, but that's a bit too much information for a street conversation." They both laughed.

"Yeah, I haven't told anyone beyond my family that I was an intern."

Esme winked. "Got it. I'll leave you to your clinic." She turned to leave again, at least satisfied with the answers he'd given her. At least knowing she wasn't totally being ostracized in this town. She remembered when she'd left Shane standing at the altar on Valentine's Day when she'd played runaway bride. How most of her so-called friends had dumped her.

When the press had been hounding the hospital, when she'd been called into the board meeting in front of Dr. Eli Draven to be questioned about how she'd frozen during surgery and her resident had thrown her under the bus because that resident had wanted to take her place as Dr. Draven's new protégé.

That was when she'd noticed the pointed stares, the whispers and seeing her name disappear from the OR boards. When patients she'd been treating for months had moved to other doctors and hadn't even been able to tell her why other than it "fit their schedule better" or "they wanted a second opinion" because maybe she was a bit emotionally scarred.

It was cutthroat. All of it, and once she'd been like that and that thought made her sick.

She'd deserved that punishment. She deserved to be alone.

But then Carson had reached out to her, handing her an olive branch. Even though it was dangerous to accept it, she hadn't been able to help herself. Loneliness had made her weak.

Ever since she'd started interacting with Carson she'd done two surgical procedures in her short time in Crater Lake. Something she had promised herself she wouldn't do. Yet she had.

He brought out something in her. Something she'd thought was long gone. Something that scared her.

It didn't have to mean anything. She could be his friend, even if she did want a bit more, but that bit more was out of the question. She didn't deserve that bit more.

She didn't deserve any of it.

"Esme, wait."

She turned around again. "Dr. Ralston?"

"It's Sunday. I just have to fax off a referral and then I was planning to take a hike around Crater Lake later. Would you like to come? You seemed to enjoy the view from my place. I thought you might want to check it out firsthand."

Say no. Say no.

But another part of her said, *You can be his friend.*

And she did want to see around the area. It was Sunday, the clinic was closed and her plans for the day involved cleaning and possibly binge-watching some reality shows she'd been recording. Nothing that exciting.

Do it.

"I'd like that. What do you think, an hour?"

"Two. Wear a good pair of shoes and pants...there's ticks in the woods." He winked and grinned, before turning and heading back toward his clinic.

"Ticks?" Esme called out, but he just waved and disappeared into his clinic.

She chuckled and headed back to her own clinic. Apparently she had to find a clean pair of yoga pants and socks that went up to her waist, maybe a turtleneck, too, and she shuddered at the thought of ticks.

There were a couple of times that Carson seriously thought about calling Esme up and canceling the hike. After he wrote up and faxed in his referral, he just sat there letting it all sink in that he'd actually asked Esme to go on a hike with him today.

He hadn't planned on going on a hike today. He hadn't planned on seeing her. Yeah, he had been avoiding her, which was a hard thing to do when she lived and worked across the street from where he worked. Even though he hadn't spoken to her, he'd seen her and it had killed him just a bit not to go out and talk to her. To kiss her.

Kissing would lead to more and he wasn't sure he could give more. He was whole again and he couldn't risk his heart again.

So Carson had kept his distance.

Then he'd seen her, blocking the way to his clinic, and all those reasons for avoiding her had melted away. He'd missed her. Missed her feistiness. Missed her smile, her laugh. He hadn't realize how lonely he'd been without her around to annoy him.

The invitation for the hike had not been on the agenda at all. It just had been a spur-of-the-moment decision really. Everything was spur-of-the-moment when it came to her. He planned things. He liked the familiarity of it. Being around Esme changed all that. He didn't plan or prepare, he just did and that was far out of his comfort zone.

Why he'd chosen a hike today, he had no idea. He didn't particularly like hiking around in the woods. He liked living in the woods, he liked working with his hands and working on his house, but he didn't like traipsing around in bear country. He liked the comforts of home. His brother and he were totally opposite in that way. His brother liked living in a shanty up the mountain and using an outhouse. Carson liked plumbing.

Live a little.

Instead of canceling on her, he pulled his hiking gear out of his office closet and got changed. If only Luke could see him now.

Luke would probably laugh over the predicament he'd got himself into.

And as he stood out in front of her clinic, waiting for her to come down, he was really fighting the urge to turn around and head back to his office, call her up and cancel.

Avoiding her was better for him. Inviting her to join him in the woods was not avoiding her. It was the complete opposite. And that was dangerous.

If he didn't see her, he wouldn't be tempted by her,

but he was made of stronger stuff than that. He could be her friend. Couldn't he?

Carson could be around her, he just had to keep his distance when he was in her presence. He had to resist the urge to touch her or get too close and be caught up in the scent of her hair, her skin and he definitely had to fight the urge to reach out and kiss her.

Turn around. Just turn around and run. Don't go on a hike with her. Don't be alone in the woods with her.

He shook his head and stood his ground. He had to do this. He was the one who had invited her and he wanted to be on good terms with the only other doctor with a clinic in town. He wanted to be on good terms with the competition, even if he wasn't really even thinking of her as competition at the moment.

Esme walked out of her clinic, locking the door behind her. She'd changed and was wearing what looked like yoga attire.

"I'm ready. I think." She spun around, waiting for his approval on her outfit. At least that was what he assumed she was doing. He tried not to stare at her. It looked okay.

Actually it looked better than okay. She looked damn good.

Carson looked her up and down. The yoga pants and jacket hugged her curves and made his blood heat.

She looked so good.

Think about something else. Don't think about how tight her clothes are. Don't think about pulling her into your arms and squeezing her butt.

He was doomed.

"Well? What do you think? Is it okay for the hike today? You kind of freaked me out about the ticks."

"Well, it's an interesting choice for a hike in the mountains."

"Yoga is all I had. Sorry, I'm not really outfitted for mountain living." Esme's eyes sparkled.

"Not kitted for mountain living? Aren't there mountains in California? Isn't Mammoth Mountain in California?"

"Yes, it is, but I've never been to it."

"Doesn't Hollywood have hills as in Beverly Hills?" He winked at her.

"You're teasing me now, Carson. Los Angeles mountains hardly compare with Montana mountains. Besides, there's more comfortable amenities in Beverly Hills."

"You're right on that," he said. "Okay, I'm sure it's fine. To be honest, I really am not the mountain man I make myself out to be."

"What? Don't you live up in that cabin in the woods? I thought you were a regular Davy Crockett. King-of-the-wild-frontier type of guy."

Carson chuckled as he headed toward his SUV. "That would be Luke."

"So you're more refined?" she asked, falling into step behind him.

"Most certainly. He's a Neanderthal."

Esme laughed. "Here I thought you two had a loving relationship."

"We do most definitely, but like all brothers we have our differences, as well. I still haven't forgiven him for scaring me numerous times when we were playing in the woods. To tell you the truth Luke was a bit of a butt head when we were growing up."

Esme laughed again and he held open the door, closing it once she'd climbed up into the SUV. When he slid into the driver's side she was still laughing.

"It must've been nice growing up with a brother," she said wistfully, but there was a touch of sadness to her voice.

"I take it you don't have any siblings?"

"I did, but he died." There was hesitation.

"I'm sorry," he said.

She shrugged. "It was a long time ago. I was raised by my father and stepmother."

"What happened to your mother?" Carson asked.

Her smile disappeared. In the short time he'd known her he'd discovered when she didn't want to talk about something she clammed up and avoided the topic.

So he was bracing himself for the fact she was going to go silent again.

Instead she sighed. "My mom left me and my dad when I was little. It's no big deal—she just didn't want to be a wife and mother."

"I'm sorry." Carson couldn't imagine not having his mom around. He'd had a good childhood, a stable childhood. His dad had worked late a lot of the time, but it had never been detrimental to him or his brother.

His father had still been there taking them fishing and camping.

He'd been there to play baseball with them and teach them how to build things.

Carson's dad was dedicated and had had a sense of pride in his work. He was a good father.

As a child he'd felt safe, secure.

"There's nothing to be sorry about. I saw my mother from time to time when she came through town. My father remarried and I had an awesome stepmother. So don't feel sorry for me. I had a great childhood." Only the hint of sadness remained as she stared out the window, as if she had gone far away.

"Sorry. Are you okay?"

Esme smiled. "I'm okay. When I say my mom left me I know the look it gets. I see the sad, forlorn look thinking that I had this horrible childhood and that's why I became a cold-hearted surgeon."

"Well, isn't that the reason?"

They both laughed at that. Then silence fell between them as they headed out of town. Only it wasn't an awkward silence. It was companionable. It was nice. As he glanced over a few times to look at her, she was looking out the window with a smile on her face as she took in the scenery around her. She was seeing it through new eyes and he envied her, but he also enjoyed it.

The look of wonder at the place where he grew up.

He never got over its sense of beauty and majesty.

Yeah, he liked the modern conveniences like plumbing, but he was glad he wasn't living in a city surrounded by concrete and fumes.

He turned into the gravel parking lot that was at the head of about three different hikes that you could take around Crater Lake. Carson parked the car. There was only one other car in the lot and he recognized it as Mrs. Murphy's. She was a seventy-year-old voracious hiker and dog walker. Her St. Bernard, Tiny, was a slobber hound and he really hoped they didn't run into them.

"Wow, three paths to choose from!" Esme slung her knapsack over her shoulder.

"I think we'll stick with the easiest one for your first time out."

"Are you afraid I can't handle the challenge?" she teased.

"No. See that truck there?" he said, pointing toward Mrs. Murphy's orange truck.

"Yeah, what of it?"

"That's Mrs. Murphy's truck."

"So?" Esme was looking at him as if he were a crazy person.

"She has a very large dog that is overly friendly and overly smelly."

Esme laughed. "Are you serious?"

"Very."

Her eyes widened. "Okay then, we'll take the path you suggested."

Carson chuckled. "Good choice."

"Lead the way, Macduff."

"Mac...what?"

"Something my father always used to say. Some Shakespeare thing."

"Is your dad an English major?"

"No. Not at all. He just really likes Shakespeare."

"I think the actual quote is, 'Lay on, Macduff, and damned be him who first cries, "Hold, enough!"'"

Esme looked impressed. "Now who's the English major?"

Carson nodded. "I liked English. I also like Shakespeare."

They started walking up the gravel path to the easiest hiking trail. One that wrapped around the lake and took the path of least resistance. It was littered with lots of benches and scenic lookouts. Lots of opportunities to stop for a picnic and take in the glorious sight of Crater Lake.

Not that many people knew about it. Crater Lake barely made a Montana map. Of course that was all going to change with this grand hotel and spa, set to open Valentine's Day.

Soon Mrs. Murphy's dog Tiny was going to have a lot more people to slobber on and it concerned him about the fragility of the ecosystem around here.

Now I sound like Luke.

They didn't really talk too much as they took the first half a mile together. There wasn't really a need to talk. It was just nice.

When they came to the first scenic lookout Esme stopped and took in the sight.

"Wow, it's much bluer up close."

"The sun is overhead." Carson set down his rucksack on a bench to stretch his back.

"How long is the trail?"

"Two miles."

Esme nodded. "It's beautiful and peaceful here. Though I suspect that won't be for too much longer."

"Very true." He pointed to the far ridge, which you could see from this vantage point. "See that clear cut up there where all the dust from the road is kicking up? That's where they're going to build his hotel and spa."

Esme looked worried.

"Is something wrong?" he asked in concern.

"No, why?"

"You looked like you were going to be sick there for a moment."

"No, I'm fine. Not sick." Then she sighed. "It's just such a waste. Such a waste of trees and beauty. I guess it's a good thing we're out here enjoying the quiet soli-tude of this place before the parking lot is jam-packed with city folks and more dogs like Mrs. Murphy's."

"Yeah, but it's good for the town. It'll be good for our practice. Well, that's until Silas Draven brings in his own doctor for his hotel."

"He's bringing in a new doctor?"

"Yeah. A private doctor to deal with his clientele. I heard that the timeshare community that's already up and running will be bringing in their own on-staff doc-tor, too, but then again that's just a rumor."

Esme crossed her arms and looked a bit shaken. "I hope it's a rumor."

"Me, too."

"You just said Mr. Draven's venture would be good for the town. I thought you rebuffed change."

"Certain changes I do, but I'm realizing the benefits."

"You don't sound too convinced."

"It'll be good."

Change had brought Esme here. Maybe, just maybe, change wasn't all that bad. Carson picked up his ruck-sack; he needed to start moving again. If he kept thinking this way he'd kiss her. "Let's keep going," he suggested.

The sun was shining, it was warm and it was Sun-day. He was going to make the most of his day off. "You ready to make it to the other side of the lake?"

She nodded. "Let's go. I'll lead the way, try to keep up."

Carson laughed under his breath. She was teasing him and he liked it. There were so many things he liked about her.

He liked the fact that even though she had lost her

mother, she didn't resent it. She didn't use it as an emotional crutch and she didn't seem dark and twisted inside. He liked her willingness to try new things. She was bright and shiny, but there was still something beneath the surface she was hiding.

Something she didn't want to share with him.

Something he shouldn't care about knowing because she wasn't his, but the more he got to know her, the more he did care.

The more he wanted to know.

CHAPTER EIGHT

"FAVORITE HOLIDAY?"

Esme rolled her eyes, but smiled. She didn't mind the fifty questions game at this moment because she was stretched out on the grass listening to the gentle waves lap against the shore of Crater Lake. She was staring up at the blue, blue sky and white-capped mountains. Only a few puffs of white clouds dragging over the peaks.

It was like a slice of heaven. Sitting here she felt small and unseen. Hidden. It was exactly what she wanted.

Do you?

Avery would've loved this place. He always dreamed of the west. Montana, Wyoming, South Dakota. Avery had wanted to be a bush pilot and work in remote areas. It was why she'd chosen Crater Lake. It would've been just the place Avery would've chosen.

A hand waved in front of her face and she glanced over at Carson, who was lying beside her in the grass.

"Hey, you agreed to fifty questions. Actually, you were the one who suggested it. Especially in light of the fact you want us to be friends."

"Sorry." She rolled over. "So what was the question?"

"Favorite holiday?"

"Independence Day."

Carson cocked an eyebrow. "July the Fourth?"

"What's wrong with that? I love fireworks, barbecues, summer. Oh, and red, white and blue."

"Most people like Christmas and most ladies like Valentine's Day."

Esme's stomach knotted when he brought up Valentine's Day. She'd used to like February fourteenth. She liked the hearts, the chocolates and the cupids. Even though she wasn't a romance girl at heart, she liked the campy fun of Valentine's. Only Avery had died on Valentine's Day. His heart had stopped right under her hands. She'd avoided the day for as long as she could until she'd met Shane.

Shane loved Valentine's Day.

It was why she'd agreed to the wedding on that day. She'd foolishly hoped she could replace a sad memory with a happy one. That was until she'd realized she didn't want to be Shane Draven's wife. They were too different. They were from different worlds.

So then Valentine's Day had become jilting day. A day of guilt.

A day she'd broken a man's heart.

So no, she didn't like Valentine's Day.

"I don't like Valentine's Day."

"Why? Most women do. I mean, such pressure for us guys."

"Well, I don't. I don't care for it."

Esme wanted to tell him how much she hated it. How she now hated the pressure, the hearts, the flowers and the romance. How it reminded her of pain and loss, only she couldn't.

She hated Valentine's Day, but she wasn't going to tell Carson why.

No one needed to know her secret shame. No one needed to know about the ghosts of her past.

"Isn't it my turn to ask a question?" Esme asked, changing the subject.

"Right."

"Your favorite holiday."

"Such an unoriginal question," he teased.

Esme chuckled. "Shut up and answer it. What's your favorite holiday?"

Carson grinned. A devious smile. "Valentine's Day."

She sat up and punched him in the arm. "It is not!"

"It is. I swear it is."

"I don't believe you."

"Okay, fine. It isn't. I'm not a romantic. I like Thanksgiving the best. All that turkey. Does that make you happy?" Carson asked.

"Yes," she said. "As a matter of fact it does."

He snorted. "This is a dumb game."

"One question in and you're ready to give up? Pathetic."

They both laughed at that. It was easy to laugh with him. She couldn't remember the last time she'd laughed like this. Shane wasn't much of a joker. He definitely didn't do PDA in public. Shane owned a successful company. He was a public figure and public figures couldn't show much affection out in the open. When they would go out, they'd always have to dress up to the nines. She would've never spent a day with him like this, playing fifty questions in her yoga clothes. Any displays of affection had been done in the privacy of her apartment or his, because he hadn't wanted the press snapping pictures.

At the time she'd got that and respected it.

She'd understood his position, that he had an appearance to keep up. There was a facade he had when he was out in public. Shane would barely touch her.

Every step they'd taken there had been press there. Photographers, paparazzi. Shane Draven was a rich, handsome, powerful man. And he needed a woman by his side. But she wasn't that woman. She didn't want to be that woman and that was why she didn't marry him.

Esme sighed and lay back down in the grass, tucking her arms behind her head and crossing her ankles to watch the water. The mirror, blue water.

"You're pretty relaxed," Carson remarked.

"I am. Is that okay?"

"Yeah, it's nice. Since I've known you, you've been on edge. Skulking in the shadows of the town trying to stay unnoticed."

"Apparently me keeping a low profile hasn't been working very effectively, then."

"No. It hasn't." His eyes twinkled. "I see you, Esme. I see you."

Their gazes locked and her heart began to beat a bit faster as he smiled at her. A smile that sent a zing of anticipation through her and she fought the urge to kiss him.

She'd thought about it before, in passing, but she'd never had the urge to just reach over and kiss him passionately. And that was what she wanted to do right now.

Desperately.

She looked away and cleared her throat. "Maybe we should head back."

"Right. You're right." Carson stood and held out his hand. "Milady."

Esme snorted and took his hand as he helped her up. As soon as she was back on her feet she let go of his hand, so she wouldn't be tempted to hold it. To pull his body closer, to let him kiss her.

That was not what friends did.

And they were just friends.

Right?

For one moment he thought Esme was going to kiss him. And for one moment he thought he was going to reach out and kiss her himself. It was hard to not reach out and touch her, to press her against the grass and capture her lips with his own, tasting her sweetness.

And he had no doubt she tasted so, so sweet.

Don't think about it.

So he didn't try. Instead he helped her up and then they continued on their hike around Crater Lake. Not that he minded the hike; it was just his mind and body wanted to take part in other activities. Activities he hadn't thought about in a long time.

Don't think about it.

"How are you enjoying the lake?"

"It's beautiful. So how did Crater Lake get its name? I would assume maybe a meteor long ago?" Esme asked.

"Well, that's one of the theories. Though no one knows for sure. They can't find a bottom at the center of the lake."

"For real?" She sounded intrigued.

Carson nodded. "They've tried and it seems almost bottomless. A local tribe, long ago, felt the lake was the gateway to another world. Of course I believe under the lake is a dormant volcano. This whole time just waiting to erupt. There are a few volcanoes slumbering in these mountains on the west coast."

"Volcanoes? I thought earthquakes in California were bad enough."

"I've never been through an earthquake." And Carson planned to keep it that way if he could help it.

"Well, I've never been through a volcanic eruption."

"Neither have I, but we have evacuation plans in town. I mean, after Mount Saint Helen's went, most towns near dormant volcanoes implemented some sort of evacuation plan."

Esme looked toward the lake. "Can you swim in the lake?"

"You can, but it's only June. It would be cold."

"Oh, that's too bad. It would be amazing to swim in. A picture-perfect lake with mountains surrounding it… it would be amazing."

"Luke told me once a monster lived in there. In the deep part in the center."

She smiled up at him. "It sounds like you and your brother had some good times."

"Yeah. We did. He was always the headstrong one. It was his way or no way."

Luke hadn't wanted the family practice. He'd wanted to be an army medic. So, his parents had let him enlist after he'd completed his residency in surgery, while Carson had taken up the family practice, not even completing his first year as an intern, to keep the legacy alive.

When Luke had been discharged after two tours of duty he was supposed to join Carson so their father could retire early. Only Luke had wanted to live up on the mountains. So their father had put off his retirement.

Carson had taken up the slack so their father would feel confident enough to leave. So that he could retire early. He worked so many long hours, nights of charting and researching. House visits and hospital visits, too, when his patients were in there.

The only life he'd known was work. He wasn't even sure what he really wanted, except he wanted to stay in Crater Lake. That much he was certain of. He wanted to live here.

It was safe.

He knew what to expect. Day in and day out it had been the same thing, that was until Esme had walked into town.

She'd shaken things up.

Now he wasn't sure how he felt. He wasn't sure of anything.

And he found he wanted a bit more.

Of what, he didn't know, but he wanted something else and it scared him.

While he was contemplating this there was a rumble in the distance. The earth shuddered beneath his feet. Just minor, though.

"Earthquake?" he wondered out loud.

"No. Doesn't feel like one. I *hope* it's not your volcano."

"Doubt that, too." Then his cell rang. He pulled it out of his pocket and recognized Luke's number immediately.

"Luke, what's up?"

"Where are you?" Luke asked. It sounded as if he was far away and out of breath.

"Hiking around Crater Lake with Dr. Petersen. Did you feel the rumble?"

"Yeah. I was right at the epicenter."

"Epicenter?" Carson asked.

"Landslide up on the mountain near the build site of Draven's hotel."

Carson felt the bottom of his stomach drop to the soles of his feet. "Landslide? Is anyone hurt?"

"Yeah. Lots of people. Some are missing. Can you and Dr. Petersen gather as many medical supplies as you can from your clinics? And can you contact as many local search-and-rescue teams from nearby towns? Other doctors. I'm trying to contact as many people up here as I can…"

"No, don't worry. I'll handle it. Preserve your cell phone battery."

"Thanks. See you soon."

Carson hung up his phone and cursed under his breath.

"What is it? What's wrong?" Esme asked.

"Landslide. We have to get back to town, gather supplies. There's a lot injured, a lot missing. We have to help."

Esme nodded. "Okay. Let's go."

Carson glanced at her. "Thanks."

"For what?" Esme asked, falling into step beside him as they all but jogged the last half mile to the parking lot.

"For jumping into the fray. I swear, it's not usually like this in Crater Lake."

"No, it's okay. Of course I'll help. Why wouldn't I?"

Why wouldn't you, indeed?

Esme had given up an extraordinary skill. She had given up an amazing talent, walked away from the hospital setting. It was something he didn't quite understand, but right now he didn't care too much about that. About her reason for running away, because she was here now.

She was here and she was willing to help and that was all that mattered.

They didn't say much on the way back to town. There wasn't much to say. Carson was trying to keep his eyes on the road and trying to think about all the supplies that he had in his clinic. What he could pack and how he could get it up to the landslide site.

When he glanced over at Esme he could see her muttering to herself and heard the word *syringes*, so he knew she was doing the exact same thing he was.

Carson parked the car in front of his clinic.

"I'll grab what I can and meet you back here in ten minutes?" she asked.

Carson nodded. "Ten. Yeah."

Esme dashed across the road. Other people were rushing around, gathering supplies, needing to go up to the accident site. Carson glanced to the south and saw dust rising from the distance and he saw smoke. He couldn't even imagine what was going on up there.

And he didn't have time to think about it.

Not right now.

Right now he had a job to do.

People's lives were at stake.

CHAPTER NINE

"HOLY…" THE CURSE word she was thinking of at the time died on her lips before it could even form. She'd been through a couple of larger earthquakes living in California, but they hadn't been anything compared to this, she thought as she stepped out of Carson's SUV.

There was dust still rising. A brown dusty cloud against the brilliant blue sky. They were still far from the accident site, but she could see the landslide from the base-camp point.

Tarps were going up as makeshift shelters and then she saw that people were being brought in. People who looked hurt, injured, broken, and it was evident to her that it was a triage area.

That was when every bit of fear she'd been feeling about this situation melted away and the surgeon in her took over. She couldn't let people suffer. She had to help.

Carson was already running toward the triage area, toward his brother, who was directing people and assessing the injured, but he was clearly overwhelmed by the sheer volume. Esme followed Carson to the first makeshift shelter. More and more paramedics and first responders were arriving, but clearly they needed help.

Luke barely glanced at them.

"Thank God you two are here." Luke scrubbed a hand over his face. "It's bad. Really bad."

"Where do you want me?" Esme asked.

"Over there, help Carson on that group of injured. I have to head back to the site and try to get out as many people as I can." Luke jammed a bunch of colored toe tags into her hand. "Tag the emergency patients with green for go. The helicopters and ambulances will take the greens to the nearest hospital in Missoula."

"Don't worry," Esme said. "Go. We got this."

Esme headed over to Carson. He was examining a head wound on a man. He was encouraging the man, telling him that it was going to be okay. He had so much empathy and compassion. An excellent bedside manner. The compassion he showed was the sign of a good doctor.

Carson was an excellent doctor. He was gentle, good and he was devoted to helping people. Just as she was devoted to medicine.

She moved to the next patient. A woman who was lying on her side, moaning.

"Ma'am, can you tell me where it hurts?" Esme bent down and the woman rolled over. Her breath caught in her throat when she saw who the woman was.

She might have run out on Shane Draven on Valentine's Day last year, but that didn't mean he'd stayed heartbroken for very long.

Six months later she'd seen in the paper that he'd married a woman from a wealthy family. A member of the Manhattan glitterati. A bit of an "it" girl.

And that was who was lying on this tarp now, moaning in pain with scratches on her face. Manuela Draven.

Esme couldn't help but scan the immediate area for Shane, because that was definitely the last person she wanted to see. Manuela Draven didn't know her from a hole in the ground. She was a self-centered person, full of herself.

Perfect for the Draven family. She looked good on Shane's arm, but Esme seriously doubted that Manuela was a good fit for Shane. Shane might have resented her time spent in surgery, they might have come from different worlds, but he was compassionate. Kind.

He's not your concern. Assess Manuela's ABCs and move on.

"My stomach hurts," the woman moaned, not looking at her. "Do something."

"Hold on, ma'am." Esme rolled Manuela onto her back and lifted her shirt. There was visible bruising on her left side.

Crap.

Bruising that fast could be an internal bleed. Esme began to palpate the abdomen and it was rigid.

Dammit.

"Ow, you're hurting me," Manuela whimpered.

"I'm sorry, but I think you have internal bleeding. We have to get you to the hospital as soon as possible." Esme grabbed the green tag, marking Manuela as priority. Where the bruising was forming, and the fact it was happening so fast, indicated that the spleen was probably involved. She would most likely need surgery.

Esme might have been able to pull off an emergency appendectomy in the clinic, but there was no way she would be able to remove this woman's spleen if needed. Not up here. Especially not since this was Shane's wife.

She didn't want to be the surgeon responsible for operating on Shane's wife.

So, Manuela had to get down off the mountain, but it made Esme wonder if Shane was here in Crater Lake—did they have one of those timeshare villas? Was she now going to run into Shane regularly?

Dammit.

It was hard to breathe and her head pounded as if a migraine was forming. That was the last thing she needed in the middle of a medical emergency.

Why Crater Lake? Why did it have to be the one place she'd settled? Couldn't she shake off the ghosts of her past?

"What're you doing?" Manuela whined.

"You're going to the hospital." Esme waved to the paramedics who had just landed helicopters at the base camp.

Manuela opened her eyes and stared at her. Hard, and there was a faint glimmer of recognition. Esme turned away quickly and rattled off instructions to the paramedics, letting them take Manuela away so that she could get the proper help she needed.

Esme kept her back to Manuela while they transferred her to the stretcher to load her onto the helicopter. There had been that faint recognition in Manuela's eyes, which scared Esme to her core, and she couldn't let Manuela recognize her.

That was why she'd come here. So no one would recognize her.

Not even herself. She didn't recognize herself anymore.

She was angry at herself, but really what could she

expect? She had to live with herself. She'd made her bed and she had to lie in it.

Esme glanced back once to see them load Manuela on the helicopter, ready to take her to the hospital as another helicopter flew over a ridge toward the base camp. Her head hurt and her stomach was doing backflips, as if she was going to be sick. Who was she? She didn't know. Not anymore.

Focus. You have a job to do.

She watched Carson, who was bent over patients, triaging them with expert care. He didn't have anything to worry about. No one would ruin his career and question his medical decisions. Esme envied him.

No one questioned him. No one would question him about his right to be here. She wanted that. She wanted to love medicine again. She wanted to feel passion about her work again. Only, she'd never have that. And she had to live with that for the rest of her life.

He glanced over his shoulder. "Dr. Petersen, can you come assist me here?"

"Sure." Esme rolled her shoulders and tried to ignore that panicky voice in her head and the oncoming headache. Right now she didn't have time for self-doubt. Right now she had to be a doctor. Esme knelt beside Carson.

"What do you need?"

"Could you look at the woman next to this man while I suture up his scalp wound?" Carson leaned over and whispered, "I think she has a concussion. She was fine when I first triaged her."

"Of course."

"Are you okay?" Carson asked. "You're pale and squinting."

"Fine," Esme said.

She moved over to the next patient. Examining her pupillary reaction and then examining her head and asking the woman questions, which she could not really answer clearly. It appeared to be a concussion, by the woman's confusion and the complaints of nausea. Esme pulled out a green tag and assured the woman she was going to get help as soon as possible.

She then moved on to the next patient and did another assessment.

It continued like that for the next thirty minutes as more injured people came into the tent. As more people came down off the mountain.

When the people stopped coming in, Esme counted up how many people she had seen and fifteen seemed like a lot for such a remote area. She stretched her back and made a round over her patients who were yellow. Patients who weren't seriously injured, patients who could wait.

All of her green patients had gone.

Including Manuela.

Which was a relief. Now she was exhausted. She was bone tired and it was hard to breathe.

Carson ducked back under the shelter, having assisted the last medevac with the last green patient out of base camp. He headed over to her.

"How many did you see?" he asked.

"Fifteen. Five of them were green. I've seen trauma, but I've never triaged in this kind of situation before."

Carson nodded. "We've had landslides up here before, but nothing like this."

"Any word from your brother?" Esme asked.

Carson shook his head. "He'll come back once he knows that everyone is accounted for."

"Do you know how many people were around the site?"

"No. Why?"

Esme shrugged. "Just curious."

She thought of Manuela Draven and found it really hard to believe that she would be up here without Shane. She was actually surprised that she was here. She didn't think the Dravens of Los Angeles would have anything to do with Silas Draven the developer.

Carson's cell went off. "Hello? What do you need? I'll be right there."

"What's wrong?"

"It's Luke. He found a man trapped under some rock. We need to take a team up there and try and extract him."

"Do you need me to come?" Esme asked.

"Yeah, if you don't mind. We have first responders here now to deal with the patients who are injured, but this man sounds like he's in a bad way. Luke will need all the hands he can get."

"Of course." Esme began to gather supplies to refresh the bag she had filled down in town. Once she had the equipment Carson took her hand and led her away from base camp and along the trail, up around the side of a cliff. It was a ten-minute hike and during that Carson was extra vigilant and withdrawn.

Esme couldn't help but keep her eyes trained on the mountain above her, watching and waiting to see if more rocks and mud would come raining down on them. It was tiring. One thing she had learned when she had been triaging a surveyor who was used to working in mountainous regions was that landslide sites were always dangerous, even after the landslide had happened. There was a high percentage risk of it occurring again if some of the debris had been caught up by trees or larger boulders.

There was still a chance that another landslide could happen and it terrified Esme beyond reason. She'd thought earthquakes were bad, but then mudslides and landslides had happened in California before.

As did wildfires.

She'd lived in California longer than Crater Lake and already she was seeing a lot of natural disasters. All she wanted was a quiet life.

When they rounded the corner, Esme whispered a curse under her breath when she saw the devastation the landslide had caused. She could see part of the new hotel and spa was being built and it had been so close to being destroyed.

Trees up the mountainside were snapped in half or simply gone. All she could see was rubble. And then she caught sight of Luke, kneeling near the edge of the path of destruction. He didn't call out to them. Any loud sounds could start another slide.

Carson and Esme quickly headed over.

"He's in bad shape and I didn't have enough of the proper supplies to help him." Luke moved out of the way. "Carson, we have to get him out of here. He has blunt force trauma to the chest and God knows how many other fractures or crush injuries. I hope you brought a chest tube kit, Dr. Petersen."

"I did." Esme knelt down beside Luke and then glanced at the patient. "Can you tell me...?" She couldn't even form coherent words as she stared down at the half-unconscious man buried under the rock.

At least she now had her answer as to Manuela's presence.

His face was bloodied, but she would recognize him anywhere. You couldn't forget the man you left standing at the altar. A man she'd thought she'd once loved.

Shane Draven was her patient.

Carson stepped beside Luke and started to help his brother try and remove some of the smaller rocks off the injured man. They could start small until Esme had him more stabilized, then they could move the larger rocks. Moving the larger rocks would mean that they would have to be ready to get him off the mountain, because if this man had crush injuries he was going to bleed out right here.

That much Carson knew.

He glanced over at Esme, who was staring in disbelief and horror at the man's face. As if she couldn't believe this man was in this kind of situation. Then she shook her head and started pulling out supplies.

It was odd for her, because they had been in multiple different emergency situations and she didn't seem to get this distracted when it came to patients. He'd noticed her withdraw earlier, when they'd first arrived at base camp. When she'd been getting her first green patient onto the helicopter. Esme had barely been able to make eye contact with the woman. She'd looked visibly ill.

He couldn't help but wonder what was going on with her.

"Luke, please tell me a medevac has been ordered here," Esme said in a barely audible whisper.

"No. The sound and blades of the chopper could cause another landslide. We need to get him stabilized and on a stretcher. Then we can get him away from the slide zone. Once we're around that bend, then we're home free."

"That's nothing more than a trail. There's no place for a helicopter to land," she said.

"The helicopter won't land," Carson said. "We'll have to hook him up to a hoist and fly him out off the trail."

"He could bleed out." Esme glanced back down at the patient, her face getting paler. "We can't let him die."

"I don't have any intention of letting him die, Esme," Carson said.

"My team is coming with a gurney. We'll have as many men carrying him out of here and to a safe, clear spot a helicopter can send down a hoist. Right now, you have to triage him," Luke snapped.

Esme nodded and pulled out her stethoscope, quickly going over the ABCs. Airway, breathing, consciousness. Carson watched her bend and listen to the man's chest. Or what she could get of his chest.

"There's muffled sounds in his chest. I suspect a definite crush injury. I'm going to have to insert a chest tube. Just like you said, Dr. Ralston."

Luke nodded. "Let us know when you get it in and it starts draining, then we'll start lifting these larger rocks to get him free."

"Was he conscious when you found him, Luke?" Carson asked. "Do you know who he is?"

Luke snorted. "Everyone knows who he is. He's Shane Draven. One of the richest bachelors on the West Coast."

"He's not a bachelor anymore," Esme remarked as she set up the instruments she needed to insert a chest tube.

Carson wondered why she sounded a touch bitter about it and he wasn't even sure that it was a bitter tone. It was just odd the way she said it.

It's nothing.

"I'm about to insert the chest tube. If he regains consciousness he's going to scream and scream loudly."

"I'll take care of it." Carson moved to sit by the man's head. Ready to hold him down, cover his mouth so that his screams wouldn't dislodge debris, so that they wouldn't all be buried under a metric ton of rock.

Esme worked fast and as she inserted the tube Shane Draven's eyes flew open and he screamed. In agony.

"Hold him!" Esme shouted. "He may be buried under the rocks, but half his chest is free and if he moves I'm liable to puncture a lung and kill him."

Carson lay across the man's body as Esme made one last twist and the tube was in place in the intercostal space. She taped it down so it wouldn't jar. The man was still screaming, but not as loud as Carson held him.

The moment the chest tube was in, bright red blood drained from his chest.

"We have to get him out of here now." Esme jumped up and began to help Luke and Carson as they pulled debris and rocks off the man.

"Oh, God, what the hell happened?" Shane screamed.

"You were in a landslide, sir. You're going to be okay," Carson said, trying to reassure him.

The man stared up at him and then past him, to Esme. His eyes widened for a moment, as if he recognized her, but it was only for a moment until his eyes rolled back into his head and he was unconscious again.

"God." Esme moved past Carson and checked his pupillary responses. "We have to get him down off the mountains and fast. He'll die."

"Last rock," Carson said, tossing it.

The first-responder team came around the bend with the stretcher and in the distance Carson could hear the whirring chopper blades as the medevac made its way to the rendezvous point. They worked together quickly, getting Shane Draven onto the stretcher, covering him and strapping him down.

Luke and his team ran with the patient down the path toward the helicopter. Carson and Esme followed them. Carson could see the thick cable drop down from the chopper as they hooked the stretcher up and secured him.

It wasn't too long until Shane Draven was secure and hoisted up; Luke had harnessed himself in to ride with Shane off the mountain. Carson watched them as they left. He turned back to Esme.

"We have to get away from this site. It's dangerous."

Esme nodded. She looked a bit green, but it only lasted for a moment before she ducked behind a bush and was sick.

"Esme?" Carson tried to touch her, but she slapped his hand away.

"Don't look at me," she whimpered.

He looked away for a few moments, until she finished being sick. When it was over she was leaning against a tree. Her breath shallow, as if she was working hard to breathe. She started retching again.

"Are you okay?" he asked again. He was worried the

trauma was too much for her, but then again she was a surgeon. A full-blooded surgeon. She shouldn't shy away from situations like this.

Esme nodded weakly. "Just get me off this damn mountain."

CHAPTER TEN

CARSON WAS WORRIED about Esme. She hadn't said much since he'd got her back to the triage area, where she was able to get some water into her and rest for a moment. He was wondering if she had a touch of heatstroke, or too much exposure from the sun. They had been working outside for a while and running on adrenaline. She'd been a trooper through it all, but they'd started working after a two-mile hike. They both had been out of breath sprinting that last half a mile before going up the mountain.

What if it was mountain sickness?

With Esme being from Los Angeles, he knew that she wouldn't be used to the higher altitude and, working as they had been on injured people, that could be the reason why she was ill. He didn't know if she'd been this far up the mountain before. They were higher up than his place or the mill.

After he'd got her settled another shallow quake rocked the ground and they heard a pop as more debris was carried down the side. She gripped his arm and buried her face in his chest as the second landslide hit. Carson held her close to him. Soothing her, and it felt so good.

So right.

When the shaking ended he reluctantly let her go and went to see if anyone else was injured.

At least this time no one was in the path, but it was clear to them they had to get down off the mountain, even if they were relatively safe on the lee side.

Only they couldn't leave. Not until all the injured were taken down first.

Esme refused to lie down, but at least he had her sitting down, picking at the label of an empty water bottle as the last of the injured was taken down the mountain in an ambulance. Carson headed over to her.

"Here." He held out another bottle of water.

"No, thanks. I just finished one."

Carson took the empty bottle from her. "You need to drink a lot of water. I think you have altitude sickness."

Esme sighed and took the water from him. "I don't have altitude sickness. I'm just tired and have a headache."

"Something is up with you. You were sick after we got Mr. Draven off the mountain."

Her eyes widened for a moment at the mention of Mr. Draven's name, but then she shrugged and looked away quickly. "You know what? You're right—it's altitude sickness."

Only Carson didn't really believe it was only altitude sickness suddenly. She was hiding something again.

It's not your concern. How can you trust her when she clearly hides the truth from you? You're just going to get hurt again.

The sting of Danielle's departure hurt, but somehow the idea of Esme hurting him made him ill, because if she broke his heart like Danielle he'd never recover and that scared him.

Only he couldn't walk away, because he cared about her.

She was going to be his downfall.

He sat down beside her and began to pull instruments out of his rucksack.

"What're you doing?" Esme asked.

"I'm going to examine you. You could have heat-stroke or heat exhaustion. I want to make sure you're okay. You know that acute mountain sickness can be serious and if it's that we need to get you down off this mountain."

Esme sighed. "Fine. Do your exam, but I'm perfectly okay."

"Right. A seasoned trauma surgeon throws up after inserting a chest tube." Carson snorted and then peeled off his fleece sweater, wrapping it around her shoulders to keep her warm.

Esme pulled his sweater tighter around her. Even though it was hot out and it was summer, being up on the mountain was a lot colder than being down in town and if she was suffering from acute mountain sickness she could get hypothermia quite quickly. That was something Carson didn't want for her.

Not after all the work she'd been doing.

Three traumatic events since she'd pretty much set foot in Crater Lake and each time she'd thrown herself into the fray without hesitation. He admired that about her. Danielle wasn't the kind of doctor who jumped into the fray.

Danielle wasn't a trauma surgeon. She was a neurosurgeon and, last he'd heard, was working on a big research project somewhere in the South.

The woman who didn't want to stay in Crater Lake because she wanted to be a surgeon was now working on a research project somewhere. Danielle wouldn't have gone up to the mill to save Jenkins's life. She wouldn't have operated on that surveyor and she would've come up the mountain, but only grudgingly.

Luke detested Danielle. That should've been a big clue to him. Only he'd been blinded by what he'd thought was love. He wanted a family. When his father had taken over the family practice from Carson's grandfather, he had brought Carson's mother to Crater Lake and they had started a family soon after.

Carson was following in his father's footsteps. Or maybe he tried, but didn't realize that he didn't have to follow the same footsteps as his father.

"You know, you're wrong," Esme said, shaking him from his thoughts.

"About what?" Carson asked as he pulled out his stethoscope.

"You keep calling me a trauma surgeon."

"I assumed you were. You said you were a surgeon."

"I am... I mean I was, but your first instinct was right. I was a cardio-thoracic surgeon."

Carson was stunned. "Why did you feel the need to hide that from me?"

Esme shrugged. "I honestly don't know anymore. Like the specialty of surgery I practiced makes a difference."

Carson chuckled. "I knew it was more than trauma the way you worked at the mill. Now take a deep breath."

He placed the stethoscope on her chest and then realized what he was doing, how close he was to her and that his hand was basically on her chest. He could hear her heart beating fast. She took a deep breath, inhaling and exhaling for him.

"Good." He packed his stethoscope away and tried not to think about touching her. He was performing a medical exam. Just because he was attracted to her, didn't mean he had to do anything about it.

He cleared his throat and took her hand to examine it. Her hand was so small in his. Those delicate long fingers. Talented. How many lives had she saved with those hands? How many intricate surgeries?

"What're you doing?" she asked.

"Looking to see if your nail beds are blue. It's a sign of acute mountain sickness." Then he tipped her head back to look at her lips. The last time he'd stared at her lips, all he'd wanted to do was kiss them.

Focus.

Her skin was so soft. So, so soft.

"What's the verdict, Doc?" she asked.

"You have cyanosis starting in your nail beds and I'm sorry, but your breathing sounds labored."

Her brow furrowed. "Acute mountain sickness? Are you sure?"

"Positive. I've seen it often enough in newcomers to the area. You exerted yourself on the mountain. It was too much."

Esme sighed. "So the solution is descend?"

Carson nodded and got to his feet. "Descend, descend, descend. And water. We have to get you down before it progresses. I would hate for you to end up with high-altitude cerebral edema."

"Coma?"

He helped Esme to her feet. "You got it."

"I clearly need to do more research on acute mountain sickness. I thought it only affected people out of shape."

Carson chuckled. "No, it can happen to anyone not used to the altitude. Come on, I'll drive you back down."

"Can we leave?"

"I'll let the leader of the first responders know. You head over to the car."

Esme nodded and huddled into his sweater as she slowly walked over to his SUV. Carson watched her, to make sure she didn't fall over. Since she had a bit of cyanosis, he was positive that she was experiencing some vertigo and dizziness.

His case of weak knees, however, had nothing to do with acute mountain sickness. It all had to do with Esme. Once she was safely in his SUV, he found the team leader of the first responders who were still at the base-camp site.

"Dr. Ralston, how can I help you?"

"Dr. Petersen is suffering from ACM. I have to get her down off the mountain. If you need me to come back, I'll return when I make sure she's stable and resting."

"I don't think we'll need you back, Dr. Ralston. All missing have been accounted for and all injured are being taken down off the mountain. If there are any other issues I'll contact the other Dr. Ralston."

"Well, he traveled with an emergency patient off the mountain. So if you need someone, page me."

"Will do. Thanks, Doctor."

Carson nodded and walked to his SUV. When he sat

down he could see Esme was shivering, trying to keep the fleece around her tight.

"Sorry for throwing up out there," she said through chattering teeth. "I've heard of altitude sickness. I just didn't think that it would happen to me. I thought..." She trailed off and shook her head. "Sorry."

"No one expects it to. Don't worry about it. Just don't do that in my car." He winked at her and Esme laughed.

"That was a pretty big landslide," she remarked.

"It wasn't. I've seen worse. Way worse." He drove the car slowly down the mountain road. He didn't want to descend with her too fast.

Esme shuddered. "Worse. That's a scary thought."

"It was. I was ten. My father spent the night on the mountain with Luke when a landslide hit a smaller town just west of Whitefish. It almost buried the entire town. Luke was fifteen and was able to help Dad. They searched for survivors. So many were lost. I just remember being terrified. Left at home with Mom, not knowing if Luke and Dad would come back and worrying that it would happen in Crater Lake."

"I'm sure your mom probably felt the same," Esme said.

"I'm sure she did." Carson smiled, seeing she could barely keep her eyes open. "You look exhausted."

"I am. I feel so exhausted. I haven't been sleeping well at night." Esme yawned. "It's so quiet here. I'm used to the sounds of the city outside my apartment. It's too quiet here."

"Lay your head back and sleep. It's okay. It's going to take us forty minutes to get back to town."

Esme nodded. It didn't take much convincing for her to lean back against the seat and fall fast asleep. She looked so peaceful sleeping that when he got close to town he didn't head for town. She needed rest and he wasn't going to try and find her key and wake her up so she could sleep alone in her apartment above her clinic.

It was better that he took her home, so he could watch over her while she slept.

Is it really a better idea?

From a medical standpoint it was. She had experienced the symptoms of acute mountain sickness. He couldn't leave her alone—what if she didn't improve? What if her cyanosis worsened?

It has nothing to do with acute mountain sickness.

Why was he torturing himself like this? He couldn't have her. He wasn't willing to put his heart at risk.

He wasn't a fool. She'd leave. She'd miss surgery and head far from Crater Lake and he couldn't follow. He had a family practice to run. He wouldn't disappoint his father or grandfather, who'd left him this legacy.

Carson turned off the main road, to his property.

Esme was pretty out of it. She barely even acknowledged him as he helped her out of the SUV and into his house. The closest bedroom was his on the main floor, so he scooped her up and carried her into his bedroom, setting her down on his bed. The sun was in the west and flooded his room with light, so he closed the blinds slightly, to darken the room.

He picked up her hand one more time to check her cyanosis and the pink was returning. The blue disappearing.

The cure was working.

Thank God.

She didn't deserve to suffer from acute mountain sickness. Not after helping all those people today. He felt bad; she was probably suffering so much the entire time they were up there on the mountain. And their hike hadn't helped much. She was probably worn right out.

At least he'd got her off the mountain.

Descend, descend, descend.

Something his father and brother always reiterated. Especially Luke during his survival classes that he taught to people so they could survive in extreme conditions if they found themselves trapped up on a mountain.

She looked so peaceful sleeping on his bed.

He wished for moment that he could join her and the second that thought crossed his mind, he knew he had to get out of the room as fast as he could or he might do something he regretted.

She could see Shane's broken face looking down the aisle at her as she stopped midway. His sad, bloodied, broken face and as she glanced down it wasn't her wedding dress that she was wearing. It was the stained clothing from the mountain, her hands were turning blue and she couldn't breathe.

Esme woke with a start. It was dark and she had no idea where she was. It was someone's bedroom, but whose? The last thing she remembered was sitting in Carson's SUV and he was telling her to go to sleep as he slowly drove down the mountain.

So she must be in Carson's house. She got up slowly, her head pounding as if she had a hangover. It must've had something to do with the acute mountain sickness. At least she didn't feel as dizzy anymore. She didn't feel as if she was going to throw up.

Oh, God.

Esme sank back down on the bed, mortified that she had been ill in front of Carson. He was a doctor, so therefore he was used to seeing stuff like that, but it was him.

It was her.

If it had been anyone else she wouldn't be so embarrassed, but it was Carson. He'd been the one to see her at her most vulnerable on that mountain and she didn't like that one bit. No one saw her vulnerable. She was a dedicated surgeon.

That's what I love about you, Esme. You don't care. You're cool as a cucumber and have a great public image.

Of course after the jilting those endearing sentiments had changed in tone.

You have no heart. You're a cold, heartless woman.

Maybe it was true, but then why had it hurt so much when Avery died? When she'd lost her nerve in that surgery? If she had no heart why did it beat so fast around Carson? She hadn't realized how numb she'd been. And he'd seen her at her most vulnerable up on the mountain.

Granted he thought it was acute mountain sickness, it made sense, but she had a feeling it was something more.

Yeah, she had been feeling exhausted, her breathing had been harder to come by, but she could work through all that. She had been working through all of that. Her stomach hadn't turned until Shane had looked at her. When their gazes had connected and she'd seen the recognition, followed by anger or hurt.

Of course, it was hard to tell if it was because she had been there. When she'd run out on him the day of their wedding he'd told her, or rather his father had told her in no uncertain terms, that he didn't want to see her ever again.

That Shane loathed her.

Hated her. *You have no heart. You're a cold, heartless woman. You could have been great, but now you're nothing. Not a surgeon. Nothing but a shadow.*

And she didn't blame him. She hated herself for it.

Of course it was hard to tell if it had been loathing or the fact she'd been shoving a chest tube in between the intercostal spaces of his ribs, saving his life. And even then she wasn't sure if she'd saved it. He was so injured. Maybe he didn't make it down off the mountain. If he died…she didn't want to think about how that would make her feel. How it would end her career here in Crater Lake. A place she was falling in love with.

She was tired of running.

She didn't want to leave.

Shake it off.

Her eyes adjusted to the dim light of the unfamiliar room. She could see from the digital clock on the nightstand it was almost 10:00 p.m., and as she padded over to the window and peered through the blinds the sun was going down finally.

Even though she'd been here since April, she still wasn't used to extended daylight hours. At least it would still be daylight out when she found her cell phone, purse and called herself a cab, because she couldn't stay here at Carson's house.

That was unacceptable.

Her purse was at the end of the bed. She grabbed it and then opened the door as quietly as she could, peering out. The main room was dark, except for the flickering of the television. Esme could see Carson in the light and he was asleep. Flat-out on his back asleep.

Good.

She would quietly leave his house and then call a cab from outside so she wouldn't disturb him; that was the last thing she wanted to do. He needed his rest. He'd given up his bed for her. The couch was long, but it couldn't be too comfortable. Especially since Carson was over six feet tall and his legs were propped up over the edge of the sofa, his arms crossed and his head at an odd angle. It didn't look at all comfortable.

Esme's heart melted. He was such a generous person. She'd seen the way he was with his patients. No matter what the Johnstone twins thought of him, he was kind, caring. A little closed off. There was a hurt buried under there, but she didn't know what.

And she couldn't believe anyone would hurt him. She never wanted to hurt him. Which was why he was off-limits. So whatever secrets he had were his. Carson had the right to his secrets, just as she had the right to hers. As she wanted to keep her hurt private, because she didn't deserve absolution. It was her private hurt to keep.

Even if she was done carrying it.

She had to fight the urge to join him on the couch, to curl up beside him and watch a movie with him. To just feel safe in his arms, but she didn't deserve that because she wasn't sure that she could give that to a man.

She'd panicked about her marriage to Shane.

That was different.

And it was.

Shane didn't understand her. Carson did, but she

wasn't sure of that. Maybe he'd resent her eventually, as Shane did.

Esme sighed. Why couldn't she have some happiness? She deserved some happiness.

No. She didn't. She had to stop having this same argument with herself over and over again. She didn't deserve Carson. She couldn't have Carson.

He was off-limits.

I broke Shane's heart. I froze in surgery. I let everyone down.

Esme let out a sigh. Maybe she should leave him a note. Thank him for taking care of her because she didn't have anyone to care for her. She didn't have anyone to sit with her or visit her, but that was par for the course.

She turned around and headed for the door. It was best that she get out of here as fast as she could. She grabbed the doorknob. A light flicked on.

"Going somewhere?"

Esme cursed under her breath and turned around. "You're awake."

Carson was sitting up, staring at her with that goofy grin on his face. One that melted her heart. Damn him.

"And you were trying to sneak out of here."

"I wasn't trying to sneak out of here. You were asleep and I was going to call a cab."

He raised an eyebrow. "You were going to call Bob?"

"Who's Bob?"

"The only cab guy in Crater Lake. You would've been standing out there all night. He's not the most reliable."

Esme groaned. "Are you kidding me?"

He chuckled. "I wish I was."

"He's going to have to up his game when that big resort opens up."

"Maybe someone else will move into town and give him a run for his money." Carson winked at her.

Esme shook her head. "Thanks for that dig."

"It wasn't meant as a dig. It was meant as a compliment." He got off the couch and walked over to her and her pulse began to race as he came closer to her. She needed to get out of here fast. She took a step back from him.

"I should go. Tomorrow is Monday. I have to open my clinic. Patients to see."

Carson planted himself in front of the door, barring her exit. "You had more than a mild case of acute mountain sickness. You need your rest."

"I had my rest. I slept for several hours on your bed. I'm fine."

He grabbed her hand and checked her nail beds. "Well, you're not cyanotic anymore. Your hypoxia is gone."

Esme tried not to gasp at his touch. He just held her hand, his thumb brushing over her knuckles causing a zing of excitement to course down her spine.

She wanted to pull her hand back, but she couldn't. So, like a fool, she just stood there and let him hold it.

Snap out of it.

"Yes. I told you, I'm fine."

"You still need to rest. You should call your nurse and reschedule your patients. Besides, after that landslide and all the press heading into town Crater Lake will be a bit overrun tomorrow." Carson let go of her hand and moved away from the door.

Which was a good thing, because if he didn't he'd feel how badly her hand was shaking.

Press? Did he just say press?

"What?" she asked, hoping that the nervousness in her voice didn't give her away. "Why would the press be coming here?"

"It was a major landslide and among the injured was some actress by the name of Manuela Draven, who happens to be married to the head of some big internet company and nephew of Silas Draven and he's currently the guy that Luke is operating on now in Missoula."

Silas Draven's nephew?

Well, that explained why Shane was on the mountain. Then it clicked in that Luke was still operating on Shane.

"Is Sha... Is our chest-tube guy okay?"

"It's touch and go, but Luke's fairly confident he'll pull through."

"Good." She tried to take a deep calming breath, but everything began to spin and Esme gripped the door handle to steady herself and for ease of access when she bolted out of here.

It was like some kind of nightmare that she just couldn't get away from. Was her jilting of Shane going to haunt her for the rest of her life?

It would be only a matter of time before someone mentioned her name and they tracked her down. Wouldn't that be a juicy story?

"Runaway Bride of Shane Draven saves his life on top of a mountain. Is a reunion in the air? Did Manuela break Shane Draven's heart like Dr. Petersen did?"

And she felt the nausea begin to rise in her again.

Without saying a word she dashed across Carson's

house and found the guest bathroom, slamming the door and locking herself inside. She knelt beside the toilet, expecting to be ill, but nothing happened.

The only thing she could hear was the pounding of her blood, like an incessant drum in her ears as her heart raced. Her stomach twisted, threatening to heave, and she could feel sweat on her palms.

She couldn't believe this was happening.

Not again.

And the only thing she could think about at that moment was to run. Run as far away and as fast as she could.

There was a gentle knock on the door. "Esme, are you okay?"

"No," she said through chattering teeth.

"Can I come in?"

"No."

He sighed on the other side of the door. "I'm worried that it's the acute mountain sickness again. If it is we have to get you to a hospital."

Esme got up and unlocked the door. He opened it as she sat on the floor. "It's not the mountain sickness. I'm breathing fine."

"All the same…"

"It's not that. It's the press and the landslide and the Dravens."

Carson looked confused. "What's wrong? Why does that scare you?"

"Oh, God," Esme moaned and buried her head in her knees, the tears threatening to come. She felt his hand on her shoulder. His strong, strong hand.

"Tell me and maybe I can help."

"You can't help me."

"Try me. What can I do?" His eyes were full of concern, his hand so warm and reassuring as he gently stroked her cheek. "Please, let me help you, Esme."

She wanted his help. She wanted much more than that, only she couldn't have what she really wanted, but she could have tonight. One night with him, lying in his arms, and he could help chase away the ghosts that were haunting her at this moment.

Esme leaned forward and then kissed him. Just as she'd pictured a thousand times before, as she'd wanted to do the moment he'd stood outside her clinic demanding that she hand over the patients she'd stolen. She kissed him the way she'd wanted to when he'd invited her over to dinner, when he'd wrapped his arm around her on the pitch-black ride up to the mill, when he'd worked side by side with her, saving lives.

It was sweeter than she'd ever expected.

It was healing, but she wanted so much more for tonight. She wanted all of him, even if it was just for now.

She could have now.

She could forget who she was for just a few dark hours.

And maybe, just for once, she'd remember the woman she used to be.

CHAPTER ELEVEN

CARSON WAS A lost man.

He hadn't been expecting that kiss to happen. He'd wanted it to happen so many times, but, of all the ways he'd fantasized about his first kiss with Esme, never once had he imagined it would happen in his guest bathroom.

It would've bothered him before, because she was off-limits. Right now he didn't care. Right now all he could think about was her hands cupping his face and the taste of her honeyed lips on his.

And then the kiss ended, leaving him wanting more.

So much more. For once he didn't care if she was going to hurt him or that she was off-limits. He just wanted her.

"Carson, I want you. Please let me in tonight." She kissed him again and there was no way he could argue with that. It had been so long since he'd connected with someone. He avoided that for a reason, because it wasn't just sex to him. Sex to him let people in. Let them see a side of him that he shared with no one.

He'd been hurt, burned, and he didn't want to let someone in, but with Esme it was different. She made him forget about what had happened to him, about when his heart had been broken so long ago.

"Please, Carson," she said, stroking his face. "Please. Just for tonight."

"Esme, when you kiss me like that…I don't want to stop. I can't stop."

"Then don't. You don't have to promise me anything. I don't need a promise of something that I can't give."

It was a way out. She was offering him a way out. He wasn't sure how he felt about it. It should be a simple matter, only with her so close to him it wasn't a simple matter. He couldn't think rationally with her so close.

It was complicated.

Why did everything have to be so complicated?

This didn't have to be. This could just be the moment.

He could have this exquisite moment with her.

For once he could have what he wanted, even if it didn't mean anything permanent. He could have this moment with her.

All he wanted was just this moment.

She tried to kiss him again, but he stopped her. "No."

"I thought you…"

"I do. It's just we're not doing this here. There's only one place we're going to do this tonight."

Esme grinned and Carson helped her to her feet, leading her out of the tiny powder room. Once they were out of the bathroom he picked her up in his arms. He'd been wanting to sweep her off her feet since he first saw her, but he'd fought against it for so long. Right now he didn't have any fight left in him.

Right now he was going to forget everything and be with her as he wanted to, even if it meant putting his heart on the line.

He just wanted to feel again.

He just wanted to be close to someone again.

Carson carried her straight to his bathroom. A much larger room, with a large shower, because he wanted to kiss every inch of her and maybe the water would wash away some of the past.

"You read my mind," she whispered against his ear, nibbling it.

"I thought after a day on the mountain that you might enjoy a nice hot shower." He sat her down on the floor. He turned on the shower; the steam felt good. "I'll have one after you."

"Or you could have one with me."

His blood heated at her suggestion. The thought of her wet and naked made him burn with desire.

"Are you sure?" he asked.

She didn't answer him; she just smiled and took off her shirt. She was wearing a pink lace bra. It was hot pink. And though he'd never really cared for that color before the fact it was on her made him hot. Then she undid her pants, slipped them down and kicked them away, revealing a matching pair of panties.

"I'm sure."

Carson couldn't have looked away if he'd wanted to. He was entranced by her. She unhooked her bra and then slipped down her panties until she was naked. Standing there, completely naked.

"So beautiful," he murmured.

She walked over to him and started to unbutton his shirt. He reached down and ran his fingers over her bare shoulders. Her skin was so soft.

Esme slid her fingers inside his open shirt and peeled it away, touching his chest. He sucked in a deep breath.

It had been so long since he'd let a woman touch him like that. He'd forgotten what a rush it was.

Only this was different than anything he'd experienced before. It scared and thrilled him all the same. He wanted Esme to continue touching him. Her hands trailed down his chest and she undid his belt, slowing, driving him wild with need.

When her fingers broached the top of his jeans, he stopped her, grabbing her wrists and holding her back.

"I think you need to get in that shower, because I'm liable to take you right here on this bathroom floor and even though our first kiss was in a bathroom I would rather our first time be in my bed."

Pink tinged her cheeks, her eyes sparkling as she stepped away from him and walked into the glass shower.

It didn't take him long to remove his jeans and underwear. He only hesitated for a moment because he didn't lie. He didn't want their first time to be in the shower. Carson didn't want to take her up against the tiled wall. When he made love to Esme for the first time he wanted it to be in his bed. Her underneath him as he thrust into her with her legs wrapped around his waist.

He wanted her to spend the night in his arms.

He didn't want a quickie in the shower. Carson wanted to explore her body, take his time and make sure that he remembered every single moment of this time together, because it could only be this one time.

The water hit him, but his body was already heated so it felt cold instead of hot. He leaned down and kissed her the best he could. She was so much shorter than him.

"I want you," she whispered, running her hands over his chest.

"I want you, too, but not here. Not against this hard surface. I want to do it properly. I want to make love to you properly."

Something flickered across her face when he said the words *make love*. As if she was changing her mind for a moment, or maybe shock, but whatever it was it was just a flicker.

So instead he kissed her as she washed his body.

When he couldn't take the touching and teasing any longer he turned off the shower and wrapped her up in the largest fuzzy towel he had.

It might have been summer, but he wasn't taking any chances of her getting cold and catching her death. Especially not after today on the mountain.

He carried her through his en suite to his room, the room where she had spent the past few hours napping, and set her down on the bed. She tried to pull him down, but he moved away.

"I have a surprise for you." He walked over to the gas fireplace and flicked it on. He rarely had it on in the summer, but tonight was special. He didn't want her shivering while he made her come.

She was grinning, lying against the bed seductively. "Gas? I thought a rugged mountain man like you would build your own fire."

He chuckled. "I'm not that rugged of a mountain man."

"I think you are."

He came back to the bed and gathered her up in his arms. "Do you now?"

"Oh, yes," she said, nuzzling his neck. This time when she pulled him down, he didn't fight her, because whatever fight he had left in him when it came to her was gone.

He was a lost man.

It felt so good to have him pressed against her. It had been a long time since she'd been with anyone. Not since Shane and even then she was never all that interested in sex. She'd rather be in the OR, elbow deep in someone's chest, than having a night of hot sex.

Now that Carson was here with her, kissing her lips, her neck, her collarbone while his hands slipped under the thick terry-cloth towel to cup her breasts, she realized what she'd been missing. It had never been like this with anyone before.

No man had fired her senses so completely.

She'd never wanted anyone as badly as she wanted Carson now.

Esme wanted him to possess her. To take her.

Hard.

This was what she'd wanted when she'd kissed him. She wanted Carson to help her remember who she was. She just wanted to escape the world for a little while, because when the press came, and found out that she was in town and was the one who'd put the chest tube in Shane, she'd never know peace again. She'd be *that* person again. The runaway bride, the runaway surgeon, and she'd sworn to herself she'd never be that person again.

She had to leave Crater Lake. She had to go somewhere new. Someplace where no one knew her name. She didn't want to leave but she had no choice.

It was for the best, but until she had to leave she was going to cling to this moment. She wanted something to remember Carson by. Just one stolen moment that she could treasure for a long time.

Something that no one had to know about.

Something that could never be exposed and ruined.

Esme sighed, she couldn't help it. His lips were tracing a path slowly down her body. She arched her back, her body tingling. Every nerve ending standing up and paying attention.

"Do you want me to stop?" he asked, his lips hovering just above her collarbone, his breath like a brand of fire on her skin.

"God. No."

"Good." He leaned over her and a shiver of anticipation coursed through her.

So good. Just so, so good.

She didn't deserve this, but right now she didn't care. All she wanted to do was feel and she wanted to feel with him. She'd been numb for so long. He opened the towel, his eyes dark and seeming to devour her. It sent a tingle of excitement through her.

He pressed another kiss against her lips, light at first and then more urgent, as if he couldn't get enough of her. She opened her legs wider, wrapping her legs around his waist, trying to pull him closer.

"Oh, God," Carson moaned. "Oh, God, I want you. I want you so bad."

"I want you, too," she whispered and then arched her back. "Feel how much I want you."

Carson kissed her again, his tongue pushed past her lips, entwining with hers, making her blood sing with need. He ran his hands over her body, his hands on her bare flesh.

"I can't resist you," Carson whispered against her neck. "I can't. I'm so weak."

"I want you, too."

She did. Badly. Right now they weren't competing doctors in town. They were just two people about to become one. Two lovely people who needed this moment of release.

"Please," she begged.

His lips captured hers in a kiss, silencing any more words between them.

"So beautiful," he murmured. His fingers found their way up to her breast, circling around her nipple, teasing.

She ran her fingers through his hair as he began to kiss her again, but just light kisses starting at the lips and trailing lower, down over her neck, lingering at her breasts. He used his tongue to tease her and she gasped as pleasure shot through her again.

His hand moved between her legs and he began to stroke her. Esme cried out. She'd never been touched there before like that and then when his hand was replaced by his mouth and tongue, it made her topple over the edge. She tried to stop herself from coming, but she couldn't. It was too much. It had been so long.

As she came down off her climax Carson moved away and pulled a condom out. "Now, where were we?"

"I think I remember," Esme teased. She took the condom packet from his hand.

"What're you doing?" he asked.

She pushed him down and straddled his legs. "I'm just helping you out."

"Oh, God…" He trailed off as she opened the wrapper and rolled the condom down over his shaft. He was mumbling incoherent words as she stroked him.

"Now you're under me. I like it when you're under me," she murmured, leaning over him and nibbling on his earlobe.

"No. You need to be under me."

"And what're you going to do about it?"

"This." Carson flipped her over, grabbing her wrists and holding her down as he entered her. It felt so good that he was filling her completely. She dug her nails into his shoulder as he stretched her.

"Make love to me," she begged.

He moaned. "I can't say no to you."

Carson moved slow at first, taking his time, but she wanted so much more of him, she urged him to go faster until he lost control and was thrusting against her hard and fast. Soon another coil of heat unfurled deep within her. Pleasure overtaking her as he brought her to another climax.

She wrapped her legs around him, holding him tight against her, urging him on as he reached his own climax. She wanted Carson. She wanted him to make her forget about all her mistakes. Of how she'd run from surgery.

She wanted to feel again. To remember who she was.

She wished they could stay like this forever, but they couldn't. Right now she just wanted to savor the moment of being with him. That she was lying in his arms as she'd wanted, as she'd dreamed.

Carson kissed her gently on the lips, his fingers stroking her face as she ran her hands down over his back. He rolled away from her and propped himself up on one elbow, his eyes twinkling with tenderness.

"I don't want to go home," she whispered. She didn't mean to say that thought out loud. It just came out, because she didn't want to leave the safe, happy, warm bubble. She didn't want to go home to the empty apartment above her clinic and think about packing it all up and leaving.

A sly smile played on his lips. "You don't have to leave if you don't want to. I wouldn't mind you staying here for the night."

"Are you sure about that?"

"Positive. Stay. I want you to stay here." He leaned over and kissed her again. "You taste so good."

"I'll stay."

"Good." He got up to leave.

"Where are you going?"

He leaned back over and kissed her again. "I'll be right back. Just get under the duvet and relax."

Carson took the discarded towel and wrapped it around his waist. He opened the blinds and finally the sun had gone down. The inky black sky was lit by a full moon and a thousand stars.

She'd never seen so many stars.

"Amazing," she whispered.

Carson nodded and then climbed into bed beside her. "You can see it through the skylight, as well."

Esme leaned back against the pillow and stared up at the sky thick with stars. "It's like we're under the Milky Way."

"Almost."

"What would make this perfect is the aurora borealis."

Carson chuckled. "Don't push your luck. Fall is a better time to see them. You'll see one then for sure."

Will I?

Esme rolled over on her side and touched his face.

She didn't want to leave, but she couldn't stay. A man like Carson deserved so much more than her.

"I want you again, Carson." She couldn't believe she was uttering those words, but she did. She wanted him again.

He grinned lazily. "I'm happy to oblige."

She cocked an eyebrow. "Oh, yes?"

"Yes, because I'm not done with you yet. We have all night."

A zing coursed through her. Oh, yes. This was going to be her undoing.

It was going to kill her to leave Crater Lake.

It was going to kill her to leave him.

CHAPTER TWELVE

CARSON REACHED OUT the next morning, but she was gone. The spot on her side of the bed was empty and cold.

Her spot.

He'd never thought of it as anyone's spot before. It was just his bed, somewhere he slept. Now he missed her and she'd only been in his bed one night.

One night and he was hooked on her as if she were a drug. This was exactly why he couldn't be with someone.

The morning light flooded into his bedroom. It was blinding and he realized that he'd slept through his alarm.

Dammit.

At least he didn't have a patient until the afternoon. Besides, if he had a patient in the morning Louise would've called him by now, berating him for being late.

He glanced over to where Esme had been, to the spot where he'd made love to her under a sky of stars, but now she was gone. His bed felt empty.

Only your bed?

Why had he thought it was going to be any different? Why had he expected her to stay with him?

They always left.

Danielle had left and now Esme. Even though he knew logically it was just for a night, that they hadn't made promises to each other, it still was like a knife to the gut. He'd wanted to wake up next to her. He wanted to make love to her again, in the morning light. Only she was gone.

His bed was empty.

It had never felt empty before.

Not even when Danielle had left. He didn't like the way Esme affected him. He was fine before she'd come to town, but now that he'd had her, he wanted her all the more.

Dammit.

His cell phone went off and he reached over and grabbed it. It was Luke's cell.

"Hello?" Carson answered.

"I called the office but Louise said you hadn't shown up for work yet."

"I overslept."

"I haven't slept yet," Luke remarked.

"Where are you?" Carson asked.

"I'm still in Missoula. The guy we pulled off the mountain is in bad shape."

"It looked like he was."

"I had a bit of a fight with a surgeon here," Luke said and then snorted. "I won out in the end. I always do."

"Did he survive?" Luke asked.

"Of course he did. Didn't you hear me say I always win out in the end?"

Carson rolled his eyes. "Do you need me to cancel my afternoon appointments and come get you in Missoula or are you catching a flight back?"

"Can you come get me? I have to get back up on the mountain and assess the damage. Plus Eli Draven is demanding a personal status update on his son."

"You mean the surgeon Dr. Eli Draven, the cardio-thoracic surgeon?"

"Yeah. That man we saved was his son."

"Why doesn't he just go to Missoula?"

"Dr. Draven was in Great Falls with his daughter-in-law. She had a splenectomy."

"They didn't fly her to Missoula?"

"No. Missoula was slammed and Great Falls had a bed. Shane Draven got in here only because it was dire."

"Why was Missoula slammed?"

Luke sighed. "Another landslide south of Whitefish."

"So how is Dr. Draven's daughter-in-law?"

"Apparently she's on the mend and he's back in Crater Lake demanding blood."

"For what?" Carson asked. "It was an act of God."

"You know that and I know that. There's no talking to these guys sometimes. He wants to speak with Dr. Petersen. I told him that Dr. Petersen is the one who probably saved his son's life. He didn't seem thrilled that it was Dr. Petersen and not you or me."

"Whatever, his son is alive thanks to Esme."

"I know that. And Esme, eh?" Luke asked, teasing. "I didn't know you were on a first-name basis."

"Mind your own business."

"Fine. So can you come and get me?"

"Okay," Carson said. "I'll shower and come get you in Missoula."

"Thanks, Carson. Oh, and bring coffee."

Luke hung up and Carson set his phone back down on his nightstand. He'd rather just spend the morning in bed where Esme's scent still lingered on the pillow, but he couldn't do that. He couldn't leave Luke stranded in Missoula.

The bubble had burst and he had to head back out into the real world, as much as he hated to do so.

"Who called?"

Carson nearly jumped out of his skin as Esme padded into his bedroom with a tray that had what looked like breakfast on it. Though he wasn't sure.

"What?" Esme asked, confused. "You look like you've seen a ghost or something."

"I thought you left." He sat up and scrubbed a hand over his face.

"I almost did, but then realized that probably Bob's taxi service wouldn't be up and running at six in the morning when I woke up."

Carson chuckled. "You're probably right, but it's ten in the morning."

"Do you want me to leave?"

"No, it's not that…"

Esme grinned. "Good, 'cause now you can get your coffee."

He moved over and she sat down on the bed next to him, placing the tray on the bed. "I didn't know I had one of those."

"What?" she asked, glancing around.

"This tray thing." He took the mug and sipped the coffee. It was good, but as he eyed the black and yellow stuff on the tray he wasn't so sure. "So, what do we have here?"

"Eggs," she said as if he should've known what the burnt gelatinous mess was.

"Ah, can I pass? I have to get up and drive to Missoula today."

"Missoula?"

"Luke needs a ride back to Crater Lake. He has to get back on the mountain. He was in Missoula operating on Shane Draven all night, the guy we pulled out from under the landslide. Did you know he's Dr. Eli Draven's son? His father is a surgical legend."

The moment he said the name Shane Draven again her demeanor changed completely. She set down her almost-empty mug on the tray and then picked the tray up. She wasn't making eye contact with him. And then things started to piece together. He just didn't know the connection yet.

"Well, then, you better get going."

"What's wrong?" Carson asked.

"What do you mean?"

"What is it about Shane and Eli Draven that made you tense? You totally changed and, come to think about it, it happened at the mill. As soon as they mentioned Silas Draven was a client, but then you realized it was someone else. It's Shane and Eli who make you nervous. Why?"

Esme shook her head. "I—I don't know what you're…" She trailed off and then set the tray down on his dresser to cross her arms.

Carson got out of bed and pulled on his jeans and then came around the other side. "I think you know exactly what I'm talking about. Don't you? Luke said Dr. Draven didn't seem too pleased you worked on his son."

"Is that so?" Her voice was shaking so bad. As if she was terrified. Come to think of it, he was pretty terrified, too.

He was terrified about how he was feeling about her.

Last night when he'd taken her in his arms it had changed. It had all changed. After Danielle had left him and broken his heart he'd never wanted to feel anything for anybody again. He wasn't sure what he was feeling at the moment.

All he knew was he wanted to console her.

Tell her that it was all going to be okay.

Only, he wasn't sure if it would be, because he wasn't sure if he was okay.

"Tell me. It'll be all right. Tell me."

Esme shook her head. "I can't. You wouldn't understand."

"Try me."

"Right," she snorted. "Look, you wouldn't understand. You can't understand."

"I think I might. I've seen hurt before. I've seen heartache."

"Really? You've seen heartache?" she snapped. "Well, was that heartache spread all over the national newspapers? First when you froze during a surgery that cost a patient his life and then leaving your fiancé, who happened to be your mentor and boss's son, on Valentine's Day? Did you have the press hounding you constantly, camped outside the hospital you worked at? Having patients suddenly changing their minds because they had no faith in the surgeon who froze? Your mentor turning on you? Your family disappointed in you?"

Esme's lip trembled, her eyes filling with tears. "Shane Draven was my fiancé and I ran. Dr. Eli Draven was my mentor. He taught me everything. I was his star pupil. After my reputation was shattered by the press, I gave it all up. I gave up surgery, the one thing I loved more than anything, because I didn't deserve it. I don't deserve happiness. I hurt Shane. Me. It was me. All me."

Carson took her in his arms. She tried to fight him, but he held her still. "I was engaged."

Esme stopped and looked up at him. "What?"

"I was engaged. She left me, because I wanted to stay in Crater Lake and she wanted to take a job as a surgeon across the country. It was my fault that she left. So I understand heartache. I get the pain."

Only she didn't look convinced and Carson didn't think that she believed him.

That was okay, because he hated himself for being the cause of his own heartache. Just as she was the cause of her own.

Esme sighed inwardly. She wanted to tell him that he didn't understand, because he wasn't the one that left, but she didn't. Carson wouldn't understand what she was feeling and she got that. No one would understand.

It was her pain to bear alone. She'd lost herself and her career. It was all her fault.

She didn't expect anyone to take it on, to understand it.

Carson and she had shared that one night together, but that was all it had to be. It didn't have to be anything else and it couldn't be, because she was leaving Crater Lake.

As soon as she was able to, she'd send her patients back over to Carson and find some other small town where she could disappear. Where she wouldn't get involved with anyone, because that was all she deserved.

When it came to Carson she'd been so weak. She'd let her loneliness dictate her actions. She'd been so isolated in Los Angeles; people she'd thought were friends had cut her out of their lives. Her father had been disappointed with her giving up surgery and then leaving Shane at the altar, and then her job had been taken away from her. It had taken her a long time to even pluck up the courage to pick up the remnants of her life and find somewhere to start fresh.

Only, her past had caught up with her up on that mountain. Everything she cared about. Everything she loved was taken away from her in the end. She couldn't lose Carson. She wouldn't even risk it.

She had to leave and when she started over, she wasn't going to make the same mistakes that she'd made in Crater Lake.

"I need to go home now," she said, hoping her voice didn't crack too much as she tried to control the tears threatening to spill. "Besides, you have to pick up your brother in Missoula."

"Come with me to Missoula. The drive will do you good."

She shook her head. "No, thanks. I have some patients to see this afternoon. If you could just take me back into town."

Which was a lie. She didn't have any patients.

Not today.

Carson looked disappointed. If it were to anywhere else, if the landslide hadn't happened, if he hadn't discovered her secret, she might've gone with him because she liked car rides. She'd driven to Montana, her car giving out on her when she'd rolled into Crater Lake.

But now she just needed to get back to the place she called home. Two days before the landslide she had unpacked the last box, thinking that she had found a permanent home. Now she realized that was just a myth.

There could be no permanent home for her.

There was no safe place for her.

"Okay, just let me get dressed and I'll take you back into town."

Esme picked up the tray and nodded. "Thank you."

She left him to get dressed as she headed into the kitchen. She rinsed the dishes and put them into his dishwasher for him, cleaning up the mess she'd made trying to make him breakfast. Totally oblivious for a moment that her past had caught up with her.

She'd let her guard down and she hated herself for that.

Esme wandered over to the window and looked down at Crater Lake, smiling as she remembered that short stolen moment down on the shore of the lake that she'd had with Carson. When she'd forgotten who she was.

She'd forgotten she was a disgraced doctor.

She'd forgotten that she'd broken Shane's heart.

She'd forgotten that she'd disappointed her father and she'd forgotten about why she became a surgeon.

"You ready to go?" Carson asked.

Esme turned and he was fully dressed again, which was a shame.

No. You can't think that way.

"Yeah."

They didn't say anything to each other as they went out to his truck. The trip to town was awkward, too. She wanted to tell him how much last night had meant to her, because it had, but Esme thought it would just make things worse.

It wouldn't be good for either one of them.

Carson was frowning as he drove, his hands gripping the steering wheel. It was as if he was holding back things to say to her.

Things, if her circumstances were different, she'd want to hear.

He pulled up in front of her building and sat there.

"Thanks for last night," she said, breaking the awkward silence that descended between them.

It meant so much to me.

Only she didn't say those thoughts out loud and she didn't think the other three words that she really wanted to say, because if she thought about it then it would hurt all the more when she left.

"It meant a lot to me, too," Carson said. Then he turned to look at her. "We didn't make any promises, I know that, but…"

She touched his lips. "No. We didn't and that's okay."

He took her hand. "It's not, though. It wasn't your fault. Patients die all the time and you shouldn't let that inhibit your career. You're a brilliant surgeon. We all make mistakes. You shouldn't leave that talent on a shelf, rusting away."

Only she had and that inhibition had cost her her career in the end.

She smiled and then kissed him gently on the lips. "Thanks again."

Carson nodded. "Are you sure you don't want to come to Missoula with me?"

"Positive. Go get your brother. I have patients."

He nodded. "Right. I'll call you when I get back from Missoula."

"Sure." Only she wasn't going to answer her phone and by the time he realized she was leaving she was hoping to be packed up, in the new car she'd have to buy, and be on the road. If they weren't making any promises to each other, then he shouldn't worry that she didn't answer her phone.

"Do you want to have dinner when I get back?" Carson asked.

"No. Like I said, I'll be really busy with patients this afternoon and I think I'll try to head to bed early tonight. Give me a call in a couple of days. I have a lot of stuff to get caught up on."

It was a lie. She hated lying, but it was for the best.

"Okay. I'll see you later."

Esme nodded and got out of the car. "Goodbye, Carson."

And before he could say anything else she shut the door and ran into her building. Only glancing back once to watch his SUV head off on the main road out of town. Tears stung her eyes, but she wouldn't let them out. She brushed them away, because she didn't deserve to cry for him. She didn't deserve to have him.

She was going to hurt him as his former fiancée had. She was breaking another man's heart.

Even if it was the best for him.

And the worst for her.

CHAPTER THIRTEEN

"Louise, make sure that my afternoon is clear. I have to go get Luke in Missoula."

"Of course, Dr. Ralston."

Carson rubbed his forehead. He'd been supposed to get Luke on Monday after the landslide, but he'd got as far as Whitefish, Montana, when he'd got a text from Luke asking Carson to call him.

Carson had pulled off the road at a rest stop and called his brother back.

Apparently Shane Draven had taken a turn for the worse and Luke had wanted to stay in Missoula to monitor Shane's progress. Dr. Eli Draven had been insisting on it as Luke was the one who had saved Shane's life and Eli had made it clear Esme was not to go near Missoula.

Ungrateful jerk.

Luke knew the chief of surgery at the hospital and was getting special privileges to stay and work there. His brother had also had a few choice words about the annoying female trauma attending who was working on Shane's case with him, which had made Carson chuckle.

So Carson had returned to Crater Lake. He'd tried to call Esme, but she hadn't answered his phone or his knocks on her door and he was worried about her. She'd probably been avoiding the press that had come to town. He didn't blame her for keeping a low profile with the media circling.

Of course now the press was leaving. There was nothing new to report in Crater Lake.

Why are you so worried?

When they'd decided to sleep together, they had both made it quite clear that nothing could happen between them. He should be relieved or happy that she was now giving him the cold shoulder.

She'd been hurt.

Just as he'd been hurt.

This was for the best. It would make it easier. No awkwardness. No expectations.

Was it really the best?

It wasn't. He didn't like it one bit. It had been three days since he'd dropped her off at her clinic. Three days since he'd seen her.

Three days since he'd last kissed her.

He wanted so much more from her. He wanted it all; he just wasn't sure if he could trust her. There was a greatness in her, something she had suppressed because she had been scared. Esme would soon discover that and she'd move on.

Carson couldn't move on.

Crater Lake was his home.

He glanced out the window at her clinic. It had been closed today, which was odd. He hadn't even seen her nurse head to work.

Is it really your concern?

It wasn't and he had to keep reminding himself that it wasn't his business at all. They were just friends, just colleagues. That was all they were. He couldn't give her more and she couldn't give him more.

Why not?

Carson cursed under his breath and tried to concentrate on the chart in his hand. He was supposed to be going over his patient's file. He was supposed to be analyzing tests so that he could tell his patient tomorrow what was going on with him. All he should focus on now was his patients and the fact he had to drive about three and a half hours to Missoula to get Luke.

He shouldn't be worrying about Esme Petersen.

Only he couldn't help himself. She'd gotten under his skin, into his blood. She was in his veins like a drug.

Dammit.

There was a knock at the door and Louise opened it. "Dr. Ralston, Mrs. Fenolio is hoping that you could fit her in tomorrow. Can I fit her in?"

Carson was confused. "Mrs. Fenolio is not my patient. She's Dr. Petersen's."

"Not anymore according to Mrs. Fenolio. Apparently Dr. Petersen is selling her practice and leaving town."

Carson's world began to spin off-kilter.

I'm leaving, Carson. I've been offered a job as Head of Neurosurgery in New York. I'm going.

Are you asking me to go?

No, Carson. I'm not. You won't leave Crater Lake and that's why I'm leaving you.

That's it? You never even gave me the chance to say yes or no.

Well?

I can't leave my father's practice.

See, what was the point of asking? Goodbye, Carson.

"Pardon?" he asked, shaking the memories away.

"Actually, Mrs. Fenolio is not the first former patient to call and ask to come back. The Johnstone twins have an appointment at the end of the week. I also have a pile of patients from that timeshare community who are looking for a new doctor now that Dr. Petersen is closing up shop. So what do I tell them?"

He didn't give Louise an answer. Instead he pushed past her and ran out of the office, crossing the street to bang on Esme's clinic door.

"Esme, open up. I know you're in there."

He continued to pound his fist against the door until she answered. There were dark circles under her eyes when she opened the door just a crack.

"Carson, I don't have time—"

"You're leaving town?" Carson cut her off.

Esme sighed. "I don't have time to talk to you about this."

"I think you can make time for me."

"Go back to your clinic." She tried to shut the door, but he stuck his foot in the gap and forced his way in. "Get out of here, Carson. Go home."

"No." He shut the door behind him and stood in front of it. "You're giving up your practice?"

She crossed her arms. "Yes."

"Why?" he demanded.

She shook her head, annoyed with him. "It's none of your concern."

"You're running away from ghosts. Aren't you? I mean, that's what you did when you left Los Angeles and that's what you're doing here."

Her eyes went positively flinty. He'd hit a nerve and he didn't care. She was running away. She was running out. Just as Danielle had and it hurt. He should've known better, but he was a fool and he was blinded by love.

He'd been blinded by her.

"It's not any of your business."

Carson shook his head. "Why? Why are you running away?"

"As I said. It's not any of your business why I'm leaving. People leave towns. They grow, they change and they forge new trails for themselves. Of course, you wouldn't know anything about that, would you? Since you refuse to leave Crater Lake. I mean, that's why your last relationship failed, wasn't it?"

It was like a slap to the face. It was the truth, but it stung all the same. He should've known better. He'd opened his heart and it was being thrown back in his face. Torn asunder again. Only this one hurt worse than when Danielle had discarded him.

"Go, then. I don't care. At least I'm not a coward. I can face what I'm afraid of. I don't run away from my problems."

A tear slid down her cheek and he knew that he'd hurt her, just as she'd hurt him.

"No, you just let your problems run away for you."

He didn't say anything as he opened the door to her clinic and slammed it behind him. It was good she was leaving.

Was it?

Carson didn't know.

He didn't know what he was feeling. Only that he

was angry at himself for opening up to someone again. For letting someone in.

For letting Esme absolutely shatter his heart.

Esme wanted to go after him, even if he had hurt her, because he was right. She was running away from the ghosts of her past again, but it was for the best. She cared for Carson. She loved Carson and she didn't want to drag him into her mess.

It was in Carson's best interests that she left. He didn't need to be associated with her; he wouldn't want to be associated with her. She was a failure.

What would that do to his practice, being associated with her? It was an old practice that had been in his family for so long. She couldn't destroy that, because she loved Carson.

It was better to get out now before she got in too deep. Before she totally destroyed Carson's career or ran out on their wedding.

Who says you'll run? a little voice inside her asked.

She didn't know that for certain, but any time any relationship in her past had gotten serious she'd run.

The only problem with running was that she was so alone.

And she was getting tired of running even if it was for the best. Even if it was mandatory. She was a coward. Carson was right. She was too afraid to love. Too afraid to lose someone she loved.

It hurt that he'd called her a coward, but it was true.

She'd run away from surgery. She'd run from Shane and now she was running away from Carson. She wasn't even giving him the choice or the chance to be with her.

You didn't run from Avery. You stayed with him.

Stayed and tried to keep him from bleeding out, even though you'd been alone, young and terrified.

Esme crumpled up in a ball and began to sob.

When had her life become such a failure?

There was a knock at her door. She wanted to ignore it. Worried that Carson had come back, because she didn't want him to see her like this. She didn't want him to see her again. She didn't deserve any kind of absolution or pity from him.

The knocking was incessant and then she heard a voice. One that she hadn't heard in a long time.

"Esme, it's your father. Can I come in?"

Dad?

She hadn't seen him since she'd disappointed him so badly, when she'd given up on surgery and run out on Shane.

She leaped up and ran to the door, flinging it open. "Dad? What're you doing here?"

Before he answered he hugged her, pulling her close into an embrace that made tears well in her eyes, but she didn't return the hug, too shocked that he was standing here.

"I can't believe you're here," she murmured as the hug ended.

"Well, I saw on the news that there was a massive landslide in Crater Lake. Your mother mentioned to me that was where you were moving to. Can I come in?"

"Sure." Esme stepped to the side and let him in her clinic. She shut the door and locked it. "I don't understand. I didn't tell Mom where I was going. I haven't talked to either of you since Valentine's Day, the day I...the day I ran from Shane."

"Not your stepmother. Your biological mother."

"Ah, yes, I did tell her." She ran her hand through her hair. "I called her for the first time in a long time when I was leaving Los Angeles. She'd lived up this way for some time and she helped me make a decision about where I was going to set up shop."

Her father glanced around the waiting room. "It looks nice, except for all the boxes. You've been here a few months—I thought you would be further along with setting up than this."

"I'm not setting up. I'm packing up." She couldn't look him in the eyes. She was worried she'd see the same disappointment. When she glanced over, when she dared to look at him, she was surprised it was concern not disappointment etched in his face.

"What? Why?"

Esme sighed. "It's complicated."

"Esme Petersen, what is going on?"

She threw her hands up in the air and collapsed in a waiting-room chair. "I don't know."

Her father gave her that look. The one that struck fear in her heart and usually terrified most criminals when he was working the beat. "I don't believe that for a second. You know, I did watch the news reports. I know that two of the victims in that landslide happen to be Shane Draven and his wife."

Esme nodded. "Yeah."

"Did you see him up there?"

She nodded. "I did. In fact, I saved his life. At least, I think I did. He was airlifted off the mountain. I put in his chest tube."

Her dad made a face, as he always did when she talked medicine, but then she noticed the worry in the lines of his face and the dark circles under his eyes.

"I was worried about you. When I heard there was a landslide… You haven't spoken to me in a long time. I wanted to see for myself that you were okay. I couldn't lose another child."

A tear slid down Esme's face. "I'm sorry."

"You should've called. I've been so worried."

"I would've called, but when I walked out on Shane you made it pretty clear that you were disappointed with me. I could tell that you saw Mom in me and that I was a disappointment to you and Sharon. I know how hard you both worked to give me an education and I let you both down."

"Esme," her father whispered and he took a seat next to her. "I might've been concerned, but disappointed in you leaving Shane? Never, but I was disappointed you walked away from surgery. You walked away from your gift."

"I froze during a surgery I knew. I froze and the patient died. I don't have a gift, not anymore."

"Yes, you do…you're a damn good surgeon. I don't know how you do it, dealing with all the blood and vein things."

Esme chuckled, her dad breaking the tension that had fallen between them. "Vein things?"

"You know what I'm talking about. Point is you ran. You should've held your ground. You're stronger than that."

She nodded. "Am I?"

"You are."

"That's kind of you to say, Dad, but I don't think my surgery career would've survived. I became a surgeon for Avery. I dedicated my life to it and then…I don't even know who I am."

"Why did you give it up, then?"

"I lost myself."

Her dad nodded, tears in his eyes. "I know, but you're strong. Brave."

Esme shook her head. Tears falling freely. "I'm not a surgeon anymore."

"Yes. You are. People make mistakes, Esme. I made a mistake on the force."

"What?" she asked, stunned.

"I shot someone. I thought it was a burglar and it turned out to be a guy who lost his keys and was just trying to get back into his own house. And I shot him. I fired. I acted before I thought."

"Did he die?"

"No. Thankfully, but for a long time I was under probation. For a long time I was known as Shooter Petersen. The cop who shot first and asked questions later. It's not something I'm proud of. It was humiliating and it took a long time to earn back my unit's trust, my chief's trust and the community's trust, but I did. There were many times I wanted to run away. Give up being a police officer even though it was the thing I loved more than anything. You gave up the thing you loved and I'm not talking about Shane because I don't think you ever really loved him."

"Surgery?"

"Yeah. You gave that up and you shouldn't have. You're a surgeon, Esme Petersen. I have the bills from your college education to prove it."

Esme laughed with her dad. "What if the town here decides to listen to the press? What if they find out about my past? What if I can't...?" Then she thought about Jenkins at the mill. Tyner's appendectomy and the chest tube. She was *still* a surgeon. And no matter how much she denied it, it was part of her. Just as Carson was.

"You put a chest tube in your ex-fiancé up on a mountain." Her father shrugged. "Who cares if your past taints their judgment of you? Then it's their loss. Prove to them that they have nothing to worry about. I think you've been doing a good job so far, helping out on that landslide, and I heard talk at the local motel that you stuck a needle in some guy's chest and did emergency surgery in town, as well. If that isn't the work of a surgeon I don't know what is."

"Yeah. I did."

"They admire you. They don't want you to leave. Do you want to leave?"

Esme shook her head. "No. I don't. I'd like to stay, even if it meant I wasn't a full-blown surgeon. I could work in this town here and be happy."

"Why can't you open a surgical clinic here?"

"Dad, I was a heart surgeon. I can't really perform procedures here, but I'm sure I could get hospital privileges in the nearest hospital."

Her dad nodded. "That's my girl. So are you going to stay?"

"Yeah." Esme smiled and looked around at her clinic. She could reform herself. She could open up a small cardio clinic here in town. There were enough communities around the town that she could get patients.

She wanted to stay in Crater Lake. She didn't want to keep running and she wasn't going to let Eli Draven drive her out of town.

She might not be Dr. Draven's protégée anymore, but she didn't have to stand in his shadow. She was a surgeon in her own right and her career would only be defined by one person.

Her.

Her dad had made her see that she was being foolish. She'd run scared too many times and she was letting people's judgments of her rule her life.

She wouldn't run from Carson. She might have run from Shane, but she understood why she had now. She hadn't loved him. Shane had wanted her to be someone she wasn't. Carson loved her for who she really was. Carson wanted her to be a surgeon.

She loved Carson.

He brought out the best in her, encouraging her when she was scared of picking up that scalpel again.

Until that day at the mill she hadn't performed a surgical procedure in so long but he'd encouraged her. He thought her skill was a gift she was squandering and he was right. It was.

Of course, she'd ruined things with Carson now, but even if she had she wasn't going to run from that pain. She was going to stay now. Hopefully in time Carson would trust her again and maybe if she was lucky he'd open his heart.

And when he did, she wasn't going to let him go.

"So?" her father said, interrupting her chain of thoughts. "Have I got through that thick, stubborn shell of yours? Are you going to stay and finish the job you started here? Because Sharon and I didn't raise a quitter."

"No, you guys didn't." She kissed her father on the cheek. "Yeah, I'm going to stay here. Even if the residents find out about my past. I'm going to stay and face it. I'm tired of running away."

"Good." Her father stood up. "Now, are you going to make me stay in that little motel until I leave tomorrow night or are you going to put up your old man?"

"I think I'll put up my old man. Of course you can stay here."

"Good. Do you want to go get some lunch and then I'll grab my stuff from the motel?" he asked.

"That sounds good, Dad, but I have to do one more thing. Can you wait?"

"Sure."

Esme gave him a quick peck on the cheek and then ran out of her clinic. She ran across the street to Carson's clinic. She needed to talk to him. She needed to tell him how she felt and she needed to apologize for the things she'd said to him. Even if he wouldn't listen to her.

She ran into his clinic.

Louise, his nurse, came to the front from the back. "Dr. Petersen? How can I help you?"

"Is Dr. Ralston in? I need to speak with him."

"No, I'm sorry. He went to Missoula to pick up his brother."

"I thought he did that three days ago?" Esme asked, confused.

"He was supposed to, but the other Dr. Ralston had to stay and monitor Mr. Draven's health. It took a turn for the worse."

Oh, God.

"Did Mr. Draven pull through?"

Louise shrugged. "I really don't know. I'm sorry. Anyways, Dr. Ralston has gone to Missoula today. I don't think he'll be back until later tonight."

"Thank you, Louise."

"Can I take a message for him?"

Tell him I love him. Tell him I'm staying. Only she didn't want to leave that message with his nurse. She wanted to tell him herself.

"No. It's okay. I'll talk to him another time." Esme left the office and headed back to her clinic, hoping that it wasn't too late for her and Carson.

She prayed it wasn't too late.

CHAPTER FOURTEEN

CARSON WAS SURPRISED that he got to Missoula in one piece. He actually didn't remember the drive to the hospital because all he could think about was Esme and that she was leaving. It was a blow. He was hurt.

His heart hurt.

He should've known better. This was why he didn't put his heart on the line. It was his fault. Everything he was feeling, it was his fault. He shouldn't have cared about her. He shouldn't have let her in.

He shouldn't have fallen in love with her, because, try not to as he might, he was absolutely in love with Esme and once again his heart was breaking. Only this time it was much, much worse.

When he got to the hospital he noticed all the press vehicles around. Not surprising as Shane Draven was president of a big corporation and son of a prominent surgeon.

Shane Draven.

That was who Esme had been engaged to. He'd read interviews about Shane and his father and he had a hard time picturing someone like Esme with Shane. Then again, Luke always said he'd had a hard time picturing Danielle and Carson together.

Still, it explained her behavior when they'd been up at the mill and when she'd jammed that chest tube into Shane Draven's chest.

If she had run away from Shane, and because she was a gentle person, she probably blamed herself. Felt as if she didn't deserve love.

Boy, do I understand that.

Maybe that was why she'd pushed him away.

Still, she's running away.

While another voice inside him said, *You could go with her.*

And it scared him to think of leaving the safety net of Crater Lake, the only home he'd known, of giving up the family practice, of changing for Esme.

Could he? Could he really pack up his whole life on the possibility that she'd still be with him in the future? How could he leave Crater Lake? It would mean that the family practice, which had been open for over a century, would close.

How could he let his family down?

How could you let yourself down?

He got out of his car and headed into the hospital. At the front desk they told him where he could find Luke, who was still on the CCU floor.

Carson couldn't even think straight. He didn't know what to think. When Danielle had left it had hurt him, but he'd got over it. The prospect of Esme leaving left a gnawing hole in him. It ticked him off that she was giving up.

Why was she giving up?

Aren't you giving up?

"Carson?"

The familiar voice dragged him out of his reverie

and he stopped in his tracks. He turned around and behind him was Danielle.

She'd changed. He barely recognized her, but it had been several years. He'd thought that he'd never forget Danielle's face. He'd thought it was so burned in his brain, reminding him of the hurt as a warning to him, but now, compared to Esme, Danielle was a dim memory.

"Danielle, how are you?" He held out his hand, but she gave him a quick awkward hug.

"Good. Luke said you were arriving today."

Carson cursed under his breath. "Did he?"

"Yeah, he hasn't left Shane Draven's side in the CCU. There were several times we weren't sure he'd pull through."

"Well, when Luke saves someone on the mountain, he likes to see a job to the end."

"Did he put in that chest tube?" Danielle asked.

"No...he didn't."

She raised her eyebrows. "Did you?"

"No. Another doctor did."

"Ah," Danielle said. "Well, whoever did did an amazing job. Dr. Ledet, the other surgeon on the case, said the chest tube probably saved Shane's life. Wish I could meet that doctor, to insert a chest tube in the emergent situation like that, in conditions like that."

"Yes, she's a brilliant doctor. We're going to miss her."

A strange look passed over Danielle's face. "She's leaving Crater Lake."

"You say that like it's inevitable."

Danielle rolled her eyes. "Come on, Carson. Even with all these new hotels and resorts going up on the outskirts of town, it's still a small town. Nothing changes. Nothing. Not even you."

It hit him hard, because it was true.

He couldn't change for Danielle, but could he change for Esme?

"Some things do change, Danielle. I'm glad you found your place. I'm happy for you."

Danielle was stunned. "Thanks."

Carson nodded and then continued on his way to CCU. He had been so angry with Danielle for so long, he hadn't realized how angry he had been and, because he'd been angry at her, he hadn't been able to move past it. He hadn't been able to forgive himself.

When he got up on the CCU floor, he found Luke at the charge station, charting and wearing... "Scrubs?" Carson teased.

Luke glanced over at him. "It's about time you showed up."

"It's a three-hour drive. I had to finish some of my own charting this morning."

Luke nodded. "You're so tied to Dad's practice."

"My practice, you mean. It could be yours, as well."

Luke shut the chart and grinned. "You know it's not for me."

"Who says it's for me?"

Luke arched his eyebrows. "Do tell."

"Never mind. You ready to go?"

He nodded, handed the chart back and grabbed his rucksack from behind the counter. "Let's go."

They walked in silence back through the hospital. Carson wasn't saying much. He was trying to process everything, process his feelings, his future. He didn't know what to think.

"So you're in a mood," Luke commented as they walked out of the hospital toward the parking lot.

"Am I?"

"I take it you saw Danielle?"

"I did, but that's not really bothering me."

"What is?" Luke asked, tossing his rucksack into the backseat.

"You are."

"What?"

"You. Why won't you take over Dad's practice? Why does it have to be me?"

Luke crossed his arms. "Who said it has to be you? I didn't force you to take the practice."

"You kind of did," Carson snapped. "You went off to the army and then decided you didn't want to work in Dad's clinic. I had to step up. Dad wanted to retire and there have been Ralstons in Crater Lake forever. What else was I supposed to do?"

"Follow your own path," Luke said. "It's obvious."

Carson cursed under his breath. "It's not obvious."

"It is." Luke scrubbed a hand over his face. "Ever since you were a kid you've had this great sense of duty. You were a good kid. I was a bit of a screwup, but you've had this sense of keeping our family's practice alive. Of not changing and it's been nothing but detrimental to you. Painful. How many dreams have you given up for the sake of family heritage?"

"You need to back off, Luke."

He snorted. "No. I think you need to realize that you're never going to have what you want unless you change. Do something for yourself for once."

Carson shook his head. "I can't."

Why not?

Why did he have to stay in Crater Lake? Another doctor would set up shop. He could sell off the practice.

"She'll walk away, she's going to walk away and you know who I'm talking about," Luke said.

It was his now. His dad had said he could do whatever he wanted with it. Even though he loved his hometown, the house he'd built, it just wasn't enough when you had no one to share it with.

As much as he loved Crater Lake, his job, he loved Esme more.

"Forgive yourself," Luke said. "And for once follow your heart. Do what *you* want to do. Live!"

Carson didn't say anything as he slid into the car to drive back home. He was kicking himself now for the way he'd left it with Esme.

She was going to leave and she was going to leave hating him.

He needed to tell her how he felt.

And he needed to tell her now.

Esme couldn't believe that she'd broken into Carson's home. She'd told her father what she had to do and he'd understood. He'd encouraged her to go with a promise that they would catch up later. She wasn't even sure if he'd be happy to see her. The way they'd left things, the way she'd broken his heart, it might be too late. The person she once was screamed in her head to run away, to not face the hurt, but she couldn't run away.

Not now.

Even if he rejected her. Even if he couldn't forgive or care for her, that was okay. She deserved it, but she wasn't running. She wasn't leaving Crater Lake.

She had plans. She was going to set down roots again

and the prospect of setting down roots and not running away was something she'd always wanted.

Even if the press came pounding at her door about Shane, she didn't care. She wasn't going anywhere. She deserved the life she wanted and she was going to do everything in her power to keep that.

She was going to be a surgeon again. She was going to make her father proud, but, more importantly, she was going to be proud of herself. No more hiding in shadows, keeping her head down.

Esme wandered over to the window. It was dark out and the stars were out again. It made her think of Carson. Of being in his arms, in his bed.

And as she watched the celestial display the aurora borealis erupted across the sky. Beautiful greens, just dancing above the lake. It made her catch her breath in the beauty of it all.

Yeah, she was doing the right thing.

If Carson didn't want her anymore, then that was something she could live with, but she couldn't live with herself if she didn't tell him how she felt.

The sound of his key in the door made her heart skip a beat and she turned around, waiting for him.

He came in and flicked on the lights. He startled to see her standing there.

"Esme?" he asked in confusion. "What're you doing here? I thought you were leaving?"

"I was, but I've changed my mind."

Carson dragged his hand through his hair and then shut his door, dropping his keys on the side table by the door.

"You've changed your mind?"

"Yes."

"Why?" he asked. "You were pretty clear today about your reasons for leaving."

"I know. My reasons have changed." She sighed. "Look, I'm not a girl who ever believed in romance. I thought I wasn't the girl for you. I mean, I ruined the most romantic holiday in the world by jilting my former fiancé. Romance and love have never been my priority."

"So what is?" he asked, crossing his arms and taking a step toward her.

"Surgery." She took a deep breath. "When my brother died I dedicated my life to surgery and when I got together with Shane I forgot who I was. I thought love complicated things and I lost focus."

Carson looked confused. "Why?"

"I don't know."

His expression softened. "I'm sorry. How did your brother die? You never told me."

"I was ten and he was twenty-two. We were in an accident on Valentine's Day. I had to put my hands in his chest to stop the bleeding. His heart stopped under my hands. When he died my mother left. I was scared to love. Scared to lose. It hurt too much, but I swore I would be a surgeon. To save lives so no one had to hurt the way I did."

"So that's why you chose cardio thoracic as your specialty and why you hate Valentine's Day. Why did you choose to almost marry Shane on Valentine's Day?"

"He insisted."

"And you agreed because you thought it might make you forget that day?"

She nodded. "Yes. I did it to please him. It's what Shane wanted. I ran from that wedding because I was tired of not being me. I lost myself. Still, I hurt him. I had closed myself off for too long."

"And now?"

She nodded. "I came here to find myself. To forget surgery, because I didn't deserve happiness, but…"

"But?" he asked.

"Then you walked into my life and my priorities have changed because I didn't take into account something that's very important."

"I love you," he said, surprising her.

"What?"

Carson grinned. "I love you. I figured that's what you were going to say, too."

Esme grinned. "Y-yes, I was."

Carson smiled. "Say it, then."

"I love you." Esme took a step toward him. "I used to run. Afraid of facing my inner demons, afraid of facing rejection, pain. Afraid of facing my own failures, but you changed all that. You changed it the moment you asked me to go up that mountain during that mill accident. No one has ever been able to change my mind once it's set. A drawback of being a cardio-thoracic surgeon."

"I thought you weren't a surgeon?" he asked.

"I'm a surgeon and I'm going to stay here. I'm going to keep practicing as a surgeon."

Carson nodded. "Well, I guess I'm not selling my practice after all."

Esme cocked an eyebrow. "What?"

Carson closed the gap between them. "I was going to sell my practice and go with you. I had been so afraid of forging my own path for so long. So unbending. I couldn't change for anyone. It's cost me in more ways than I care to admit. I used different excuses to keep me here, but when you said you were leaving it…I couldn't bear to live without you. I will change for you. I'd give up anything to be with you. Without you, this isn't my home. You're my home."

Esme couldn't hold back the tears. No apologies were needed. Nothing further needed to be said. She wrapped her arms around him and he held her, but only for a moment until he picked her up, kissing her. Kissing away the tears that were not tears of sadness, but joy.

"I love you, Esme. I love you and I can't live without you. You're my everything." Carson brushed away a tear with his thumb.

"I love you, too. I'm tired of running. I don't want to run. I'm in this for the long haul."

Carson kissed her again, making her weak in the knees, making her melt into his arms. He scooped her up in his arms and carried her into his bedroom.

And she was never going to let him go.

She was done running. She was done hiding.

This was her home.

She was home.

EPILOGUE

February 13th

"THIS BETTER NOT be a Valentine's Day thing," Esme said as Carson covered her eyes and led her into the house. "I don't like Valentine's Day."

"I know. I know, but it's not Valentine's Day. It's the thirteenth and it's a Friday. Does Friday the thirteenth hold any kind of dark secrets for you?" Carson asked.

"Well, this one time at this summer camp…" she teased.

"Ha-ha. Don't tease about that. That movie scared the living daylights out of me."

"Hey, you're the one who is leading a surprise on a Friday the thirteenth. Not me. And how did I not know that you didn't like horror movies? I'm shocked."

"You do?" Carson asked.

"I do. Does that change things?" She tried to suppress the laughing.

"Well." He removed his hands and Esme gasped when she saw the spread laid out for them. They were at home and there was a new dining-room table set up, overlooking the floor-to-ceiling windows at the back of the house.

The fire was snapping and crackling in the large central fireplace, and there were candles and roses everywhere.

"Oh, my gosh," she gasped.

"So, you see, the love of horror movies might just change my mind." There was a twinkle in his eyes.

Esme laughed. "Oh, come on. It's just a minor thing."

"Well, maybe this will change your mind with associating February thirteenth as an unlucky day or a day that has to do with axe-wielding, hockey-mask-wearing monsters."

"A nice dinner? For sure." Then she gasped as he dropped to one knee. "What're you doing?"

"Giving you a good memory, I hope." He pulled out a ring. "Will you marry me, Esme?"

Tears filled her eyes. She'd never expected to get engaged again. She hadn't planned on it, but that had all changed the moment she'd met Dr. Carson Ralston. And since the summer, she'd been patiently waiting for him to ask her.

Actually, she'd planned to ask him tomorrow. On Valentine's Day. Only this time she wasn't trying to bury a painful memory with something that *could* be happy. She knew that Carson was the one. She knew that their lifetime together *would* be happy.

Esme had only been certain about surgery in her life, never in matters of the heart, but when she'd foolishly almost walked away from Carson last summer, she'd known that he held her heart. He was meant for her.

She'd found herself and her place was in his arms. The thought of losing him was more than she could bear. She wanted to be his wife more than anything, to share her life with him and only him.

She'd just thought that she would have to do the proposing. And she was okay with that, but this was so much better.

This was almost too much for her heart to handle and she thought she was going to burst. She wiped away the tears and didn't care if they smudged her mascara. She wanted a clearer look at Carson, down on one knee holding out a diamond ring, which sparkled in the firelight.

How could she ever have contemplated leaving Crater Lake? Leaving him?

"Well? Your silence is kind of worrying me." His brow furrowed. "Was this too much?"

"Yes," she whispered.

"Yes, too much, or yes…?"

Esme sobbed happily, dropping to her knees to kiss him. "Yes. I'll marry you."

He cupped her face in his hands and kissed her. "You had me worried there."

"I'm sorry. I couldn't believe you were actually asking me there for a moment."

"Can't you?"

Esme laughed. "I'm sorry, but I have to say you've ruined Valentine's Day for me."

"What?" he asked. "How could I have ruined Valentine's Day for you? This isn't even Valentine's Day. I didn't even buy a single rose."

"I was planning to propose to you at the Valentine's gala tomorrow night. I even had a dress and everything."

Carson threw his head back and laughed. "For real?"

She nodded. "Your brother was in on it."

"What? How did you manage to pull that off? He's not one for romance either."

Esme shrugged. "I have my ways."

"So what did the dress look like?" he asked huskily.

"Would you like me to model it later for you?" Her pulse began to race and she wrapped her arms around his neck, nibbling on that sensitive spot by his earlobe that she had discovered soon after they'd moved in together.

"You can model for me later, but not the dress. I couldn't care less about the dress."

She laughed. "Can I have my ring now?"

"Hmm, I don't know. Maybe I do want you to get down on one knee and propose to me," he said, teasing her.

"Do you want me to slug you?" She kissed him quickly on the lips. "Will you marry me, Dr. Ralston?"

"Let me think…" Esme punched him on the arm and he laughed. "Of course, you foolish girl."

"You had me worried there for a fraction of a second." She winked.

"Well, I want to make you work for it." Carson slipped the ring on her finger and kissed her, a kiss that melted her down to her very core. "I love you, Esme Petersen. With all my heart. There isn't anyone else in this world that's meant for me. It's you I want. Only you."

"Even if I spend countless hours in an OR a couple hours from home?"

"Even then. I love you."

"And I love you, too, Carson." She kissed him again and then whispered against his neck, "With all my heart, too."

And she did. Absolutely and completely love him. Only him.

* * * * *

MILLS & BOON®
Hardback – February 2016

ROMANCE

Leonetti's Housekeeper Bride	Lynne Graham
The Surprise De Angelis Baby	Cathy Williams
Castelli's Virgin Widow	Caitlin Crews
The Consequence He Must Claim	Dani Collins
Helios Crowns His Mistress	Michelle Smart
Illicit Night with the Greek	Susanna Carr
The Sheikh's Pregnant Prisoner	Tara Pammi
A Deal Sealed by Passion	Louise Fuller
Saved by the CEO	Barbara Wallace
Pregnant with a Royal Baby!	Susan Meier
A Deal to Mend Their Marriage	Michelle Douglas
Swept into the Rich Man's World	Katrina Cudmore
His Shock Valentine's Proposal	Amy Ruttan
Craving Her Ex-Army Doc	Amy Ruttan
The Man She Could Never Forget	Meredith Webber
The Nurse Who Stole His Heart	Alison Roberts
Her Holiday Miracle	Joanna Neil
Discovering Dr Riley	Annie Claydon
His Forever Family	Sarah M. Anderson
How to Sleep with the Boss	Janice Maynard

0116 GEN STD HB

MILLS & BOON®
Large Print – February 2016

ROMANCE

Claimed for Makarov's Baby	Sharon Kendrick
An Heir Fit for a King	Abby Green
The Wedding Night Debt	Cathy Williams
Seducing His Enemy's Daughter	Annie West
Reunited for the Billionaire's Legacy	Jennifer Hayward
Hidden in the Sheikh's Harem	Michelle Conder
Resisting the Sicilian Playboy	Amanda Cinelli
Soldier, Hero...Husband?	Cara Colter
Falling for Mr December	Kate Hardy
The Baby Who Saved Christmas	Alison Roberts
A Proposal Worth Millions	Sophie Pembroke

HISTORICAL

Christian Seaton: Duke of Danger	Carole Mortimer
The Soldier's Rebel Lover	Marguerite Kaye
Return of Scandal's Son	Janice Preston
The Forgotten Daughter	Lauri Robinson
No Conventional Miss	Eleanor Webster

MEDICAL

Hot Doc from Her Past	Tina Beckett
Surgeons, Rivals...Lovers	Amalie Berlin
Best Friend to Perfect Bride	Jennifer Taylor
Resisting Her Rebel Doc	Joanna Neil
A Baby to Bind Them	Susanne Hampton
Doctor...to Duchess?	Annie O'Neil

MILLS & BOON®
Hardback – March 2016

ROMANCE

The Italian's Ruthless Seduction	Miranda Lee
Awakened by Her Desert Captor	Abby Green
A Forbidden Temptation	Anne Mather
A Vow to Secure His Legacy	Annie West
Carrying the King's Pride	Jennifer Hayward
Bound to the Tuscan Billionaire	Susan Stephens
Required to Wear the Tycoon's Ring	Maggie Cox
The Secret That Shocked De Santis	Natalie Anderson
The Greek's Ready-Made Wife	Jennifer Faye
Crown Prince's Chosen Bride	Kandy Shepherd
Billionaire, Boss...Bridegroom?	Kate Hardy
Married for their Miracle Baby	Soraya Lane
The Socialite's Secret	Carol Marinelli
London's Most Eligible Doctor	Annie O'Neil
Saving Maddie's Baby	Marion Lennox
A Sheikh to Capture Her Heart	Meredith Webber
Breaking All Their Rules	Sue MacKay
One Life-Changing Night	Louisa Heaton
The CEO's Unexpected Child	Andrea Laurence
Snowbound with the Boss	Maureen Child

0216 GEN STD HB

MILLS & BOON®
Large Print – March 2016

ROMANCE

A Christmas Vow of Seduction	Maisey Yates
Brazilian's Nine Months' Notice	Susan Stephens
The Sheikh's Christmas Conquest	Sharon Kendrick
Shackled to the Sheikh	Trish Morey
Unwrapping the Castelli Secret	Caitlin Crews
A Marriage Fit for a Sinner	Maya Blake
Larenzo's Christmas Baby	Kate Hewitt
His Lost-and-Found Bride	Scarlet Wilson
Housekeeper Under the Mistletoe	Cara Colter
Gift-Wrapped in Her Wedding Dress	Kandy Shepherd
The Prince's Christmas Vow	Jennifer Faye

HISTORICAL

His Housekeeper's Christmas Wish	Louise Allen
Temptation of a Governess	Sarah Mallory
The Demure Miss Manning	Amanda McCabe
Enticing Benedict Cole	Eliza Redgold
In the King's Service	Margaret Moore

MEDICAL

Falling at the Surgeon's Feet	Lucy Ryder
One Night in New York	Amy Ruttan
Daredevil, Doctor...Husband?	Alison Roberts
The Doctor She'd Never Forget	Annie Claydon
Reunited...in Paris!	Sue MacKay
French Fling to Forever	Karin Baine

MILLS & BOON®

Why shop at millsandboon.co.uk?

Each year, thousands of romance readers find their perfect read at millsandboon.co.uk. That's because we're passionate about bringing you the very best romantic fiction. Here are some of the advantages of shopping at www.millsandboon.co.uk:

* **Get new books first**—you'll be able to buy your favourite books one month before they hit the shops

* **Get exclusive discounts**—you'll also be able to buy our specially created monthly collections, with up to 50% off the RRP

* **Find your favourite authors**—latest news, interviews and new releases for all your favourite authors and series on our website, plus ideas for what to try next

* **Join in**—once you've bought your favourite books, don't forget to register with us to rate, review and join in the discussions

Visit **www.millsandboon.co.uk**
for all this and more today!